CW00403469

Copyright © Oliver Lea 2022

The right of Oliver Lea to be identified as the Author of the Work has been asserted by him in accordance with the Copyright, Designs and Patents Act 1988.

All rights reserved. No part of this publication may be reproduced, stored in a retrieval system, or transmitted, in any form or by any means without the prior written permission of the Author, nor be otherwise circulated in any form of binding or cover other than that in which it is published and without similar conditions being imposed on the subsequent purchaser.

All characters in this publication are fictitious and any resemblance to real persons, living or dead is purely coincidental.

Do You Get What You Pray For

By Oliver Lea

Originally written for Lou on your 40th birthday
My love and inspiration
I hope this book doesn't ruin goat-yoga for you

The cover art was designed by Ukranian artist Martellia
Serhyenkova only a week before the Russian invasion. No horror
story can compare with the experiences of the Ukranian people at
this time. I've remained in touch with Martellia, and at the time of
publication she remains safe and well in Kyiv.

Prologue

Scapegoat stood outside the door, listening to the struggling on the other side. The scraping and shuffling intensified, like the sound of someone who believed she had a chance. He took a breath, savouring the doomed hope of his victim. Then he opened the door and entered.

The woman's hands were bound above her head by a cord. She froze immediately as Scapegoat stepped in. With her arms raised, her baggy sweater hung loosely. In the dim candlelight it looked like the cap of a mushroom atop the stem of her waist and skinny jeans. Streaks of dried mascara trickled out from under a cloth tied around her head, covering her eyes.

Scapegoat walked past her to the thin brown curtains drawn over the window. Making a gap with his finger, he peered out and saw that there was some pink in the sky over the trees.

"What are you going to do?" The woman's voice was cracked and weak.

With a few strides, he was in front of her. His loose sleeve slipped up his arm as he reached up and then pulled the blindfold off her head. Her puffy red eyes blinked rapidly, focusing on him. She cried out at the sight.

He quickly put a finger up to the stiff mouth of the black goat's-head mask he wore and shook his head.

"There isn't much time. Morning is almost here. Then it will be time for me to go."

The woman's face was pale, slightly green even, her short blonde hair slick against her skin. Her eyes flicked to him and away again repeatedly.

"Please don't hurt me," she said. "I haven't done anything. I won't say a word. Please."

Scapegoat exhaled heavily, the breath resonating inside the mask. He reached into the deep pocket of his long black coat, his eyes never leaving her face.

"We will see," he said, pulling a long, slender knife from his pocket. She immediately tried to squirm away, but the metal ceiling hook to which her hands were tied would not yield. "Are you still certain you have no guilt?"

"I don't know what you mean," she wailed. "Why are you doing this? I don't know what I've done!"

"You will know." Scapegoat brought a hand up to her throat and gripped her firmly. She stopped struggling and stared at him with wide, terrified eyes. "Soon you will come face to face with the one you wronged."

"I'm sorry," she choked. "Who? Tell them I'm sorry. I don't know what I've done, but I'm sorry. I just want to go home."

Scapegoat removed his hand and stepped away. Those two words carried so little power on the lips of the cruel. "Say it again. Maybe you will be heard."

"I'm sorry. Seriously, I'm sorry. I'm so sorry. Please, forgive me, I didn't mean to offend…"

"Not like that," Scapegoat said. "Just the two words. Over and over, until it's enough."

"Sorry, I'm sorry." She straightened up on her shaky legs and stared at the ground. "I'm sorry. I'm sorry. I'm sorry."

Scapegoat returned to the window as she continued. He pulled the curtains open and the flickering candlelight swelled into the orange glow of the streetlamps. He looked down at the narrow path behind the overgrown garden which led into the woods. Behind him, her penitent mantra continued: steady, determined and tragically hopeful.

"...I'm sorry, I'm sorry..."

Lunging away from the window, he lashed out his hand and gripped her throat once again with his left hand. She yelped and coughed.

"Don't stop," he said. "Keep going. Perhaps you may yet save yourself."

She closed her eyes and forced her strangled voice to continue. "I'm sorry, I'm sorry, I'm sorry."

Scapegoat grasped her chin, keeping her face raised so as to hide the knife creeping up in his other hand. He angled the tip of it towards the base of her throat, just above the jugular notch. He increased the pressure of his grip and her words became raspier, less distinct.

"Don't stop," he said. "Morning will be here soon."

She squeezed her eyes closed and recited the words more quickly. Scapegoat felt the heightened pulse against the crook of his thumb. He'd seen this before: seen how with every apology, plea or protest of innocence, the more the words seemed to slip into meaninglessness. He saw they distorted and twisted from this young woman's lips. Anger filled him.

His right hand jerked forwards. Her eyes shot open wide and her mouth popped opened in a gasp. Scapegoat released her, stepped away and looked at the blood trickling from a small puncture wound in her throat.

"Keep going," he said.

She shook her head and her body quivered. With effort, she continued repeating those words as best as she was able. "I'm sorry, I'm sorry, I'm sorry…"

As Scapegoat stood in silence, her voice broke down into garbles. Soon her words were barely intelligible. She was pale and glistening with sweat, twitching and jerking sporadically.

Time passed unmeasured. The lamplight from the window was replaced with the palid glow of dawn. The woman hung limp. It had been a while since the last voluntary utterance had passed her lips.

Scapegoat moved towards her and lifted a hand to hold the cord around her wrists.

"It wasn't enough," he said. With a slash of the knife, he sent her tumbling onto the bare floorboards.

Chapter 1 (The Previous Day)

Alma recoiled from the hand which landed heavily on her arm. A gasp scoured her throat, which was raw from a scream. The window chilled her shoulder, and her bag dug into her hip as she squirmed away. Her grasping hand examined the base of her own throat

"What's the matter?" The person in the seat next to her asked, withdrawing his hand.

She blinked at the thin-haired middle-aged man. Turning her head, she noticed the family across the carriage aisle staring at her. Lastly, she focused on the young blonde woman sitting opposite her, wide-eyed and shaking with fright.

Alma steadied her breathing and leaned forward. The rumbling of the train slowly grounded her, and she tried not to hear the muttering of the other people on the train.

"What happened?"

"Is she alright?"

"I'm fine," she said to nobody in particular, her cheeks burning. "I'm sorry. I was sleeping. I must have....I'm sorry."

In the seat opposite, the blonde girl's horrified gape twisted into a scowl. "Fucking psycho!" she snarled, grabbing her backpack and thrusting herself towards the aisle to find another seat.

Alma kept her gaze down and swallowed heavily. Her hand went to her throat again, then slipped down to pinch at the cluster of pendants hanging around her neck. *Everything was ok.*

"Do you need something to drink?" The man next to her was still turned towards her in his seat.

"No. Thank you." Alma shook her head quickly. "What was the last station?"

"Dovey Junction."

Good. Not much further. All she could think about was getting off this train. She settled against the window and gazed out over the sandy estuary, wishing herself on the far side, away from the murmuring in the carriage.

That was the first time it had happened in public since she was a child: the first time in months it had happened *at all*.

When they reached the next station, Alma stood up and collected her things from the overhead compartment. The man next to her folded his hands in his lap and leaned away from her, perhaps meaning to be helpful.

Her final stop was still fifteen minutes away, but she couldn't sit still any longer. She made her way to the vestibule and stood in front of the door, her hand just above the 'open' button. Torrents of greenery blurred by the window before being gulped down by the blackness of a tunnel. Alma was confronted by her own reflection in the glass; the fright had turned her pale. With her dyed ash-silver hair and black sweater, she looked like a ghostly disembodied head floating in the dark outside.

The verdant backdrop returned as the train emerged. The next set of inner doors hissed opened, and a young man in a hoodie and a sports bag appeared beside her. He leaned against the wall and crossed one leg over the other, patting his thigh excitedly. Alma watched his hand. She remembered that feeling from when she'd moved away from home for the first time.

"You going to the uni?" the man asked. Alma met his gaze and saw immediately that he had both mistaken the intent of her glance and wrongly assumed she was his age.

"Not much else to be coming this way for," she said. "You, same?"

The man grinned out the window like a king surveying his land. "Yeah. Can't wait. I'll walk with you and help with your bags if you like. The hill up to the campus is brutal."

Alma pulled her backpack further up her shoulder. "Thanks, but I managed it alright eight years ago. I'm sure it's not gotten any steeper since then."

The young man's stride was visibly broken. His head nodded lower until he was once again a prince of no domain, but a new student out of his depth.

The train began to slow. As soon as the red-brick station settled in the frame of the window and the button on the door turned green, Alma swatted it hurriedly. Crossing the platform, the smell of oil and wet footprints on vinyl floors yielded to the salty coastal air. Outside, the road ran uphill to her right, just as steeply as she remembered, and more gently down towards the seafront to her left.

She took her phone out and considered the reminder of the three calls she'd rejected from Filip. It was still early, and she could see from the way the device shook in her hand that her nerves were far from settled. She turned left, towards the promenade.

The cold sea breeze and the crying of gulls had always made her feel at home. Crossing the road to lean against the sea wall, she turned and regarded how the town was laid out like a montage of history: the eighteenth-century sandstone gothic building of the Old College, the rows of pastel coloured victorian townhouses along the seafront, and the extravagant neon signage of the student nightclub on the pier. The southern peak of the bay rose up sharply to cliffs, atop which was the ruin of an early medieval chapel.

As she took in the familiar vista, Alma was only half aware of her hand floating up to rub her throat again. She closed her eyes and let it linger there a moment. As though the evidence of her own fingertips was not enough, she assured herself there was nothing there. No bleeding wound as she'd seen before waking.

The cold stone against her back and the soft crashing of the waves calmed her to the point where a coffee could see her right. Most of the students travelling on the train would have made their way up the hill rather than down; she would be unlucky to run into anyone who had witnessed her embarrassing scene.

Turning from the middle of the bay into the town centre, it didn't take her long to find a cafe on Great Darkgate Street. Most of the people she passed were seaside retirees, but she didn't feel too conspicuous with her luggage, dark clothes and piercings. The density of pubs and clubs on every street were a reminder that this was, above all, a university town, with all the vibrancy and eclecticism that came with it.

While she waited for her coffee, Alma spotted a noticeboard near the counter. The largest feature was an advert for seasonal staff, but there were a few other small cards offering cleaning services, selling furniture items or seeking members for clubs and societies, and a lot of blank space where Alma knew there would recently have

16

been cards offering rooms to let. It was the worst time of year to be looking for accommodation.

Leaving the shop with only the small achievement of an *espresso con panna*, Alma left the high street and meandered slowly uphill past self-styled dive bars and speakeasies. Wherever she saw an index card or a notice stuck in a window, she stopped in the hope that someone might still have a room going spare.

After her eighth false hope transpired to be a poster soliciting players for tabletop roleplaying games, she caught a glimpse of a figure passing across the end of the street. Even from afar, there was something about the profile of his face that roused a memory. Or maybe it was just paranoia. She had been away for so long, there was unlikely to be anyone here she would remember.

She picked up her bags and walked up to the turning the figure had taken, which led back down towards the seafront. She could see him walking briskly, hands in the pockets of his brown leather jacket in a way that was familiar, though she could no longer see his face. He was too far away for her to catch him without running and drawing attention to herself, which she preferred to avoid.

She turned into a street that would rejoin the main road on the hill and would take her to the university campus. Yet after the first step, a dissonance rang in the back of her mind. If she told herself now that the man wasn't who she thought, she'd be telling it to herself over and over again for weeks.

Better to prove to herself that it was her mind playing tricks, and have peace of mind for it later.

Alma carefully modulated her pace so that she was not too obviously rushing by the time she got back down onto the promenade. Looking left and right, she tried her best to appear lost rather than like she was looking for someone. It was a wasted performance: the man had disappeared.

She set down her bag and sighed. The short dash had left her unduly breathless. She brought a hand up to her chest, closed her eyes and tried to clear her mind for a moment. When she opened her eyes, her hand had slid up of its own accord to rub at her collar. She immediately dropped it to her side and grabbed up her bag.

Turning around, the road she'd just come down, viewed from the bottom, seemed dispiritingly long. She steeled herself, remembering how she'd tackled this hill most weekdays for three years running once upon a time. Often with a crashing hangover.

The window next to her caught her eye. It was dominated by a crowded display of crystal and pewter figurines, trinket boxes decorated with runes, incense holders and a plenitude of smoking paraphernalia. She took a step back and craned her neck to read the name of the shop.

Arcana.

Sensing an opportunity for a distraction and a way to kill a little more time before heading up the hill, she circled around to the front. The window there was equally densely packed.. A 'closed' sign was barely visible in the door window through a mess of event flyers, yet the door looked slightly unseated in its frame. Was it possible the people inside had just forgotten to turn the sign?

18

A slight push was enough to open the door, red paint flaking under her fingers. A bell jangled and Alma stepped into a cluttered room lit only by star-shaped lanterns and the heady scent of incense. There seemed to be little order to the displays, with items racked haphazardly on shelves and heaped on the floor. Several large trunks and boxes and a giant brass Buddha took up too much of the limited space.

The fragrance and gloom were inviting, but nobody appeared in response to the bell rang or her voice when she called out. She told herself she was doing no harm just looking around. Yet with each step, her discomfort at potentially trespassing grew and she wondered if it would be better to come back later. She craned her neck to look over the counter, where an opening led into the back.

"Hello?"

The reply came unexpectedly from behind her, making her jolt and whirl on the spot.

"I see you're still into this sort of thing," a man said in a soft, velvety voice.

Alma squinted at the figure silhouetted in the doorway. "The door was open. I was just looking around."

"Don't worry, I don't work here." The man stepped closer. "I just saw you go in. I thought it was you."

The door closed behind him, shutting out most of the sunlight and bringing his features into focus. Alma's eyes widened in shock as her gaze was drawn to a spot at the base of his throat.

"Oh my God...Ryan?"

Chapter 2

"Are you sure I can't carry that for you?" Ryan asked for the third time, indicating her large bag as they ambled along the seafront road towards the town centre.

"I'm fine, honestly," she said. Every time he faced her, Alma's gaze snapped to the white clerical collar of his black shirt. His face had hardly aged, and he had the same swept brown hair she'd last seen him with. The only change that eight years had wrought upon him was a piece of plastic that clipped under his shirt collar.

Yet what a change it was.

Ryan nodded and slipped his hands back into his jacket pockets. "Last time I saw your dad he said you were living in Manchester. You were doing a PhD?"

"Yes, Art History and Visual Studies," Alma said. "It's funny, though. I speak to my parents pretty often. I never heard anything about you becoming a *priest*."

"I suppose that must seem odd." Ryan grimaced. "It actually happened fairly quickly. I already had the philosophy degree and, you know, I could see that my luck with women wasn't getting any better so it seemed like a sensible way to go."

Ryan tilted his head towards her and offered a grin, which she did not return. He looked away and added, "That was a joke."

"I know," Alma said. "I wasn't waiting for permission to laugh."

Beyond the sea-wall, the waves remarked in hushed voices at the two of them walking slowly in step.

"So what brings you back down here?" Ryan asked.

"I got a job at the university. What about you? What finally compelled you to leave Anglesea?"

"That's just how it works. You don't really get to choose where the Church puts you. This is where the vacancy was ."

"Really?" Alma gave him a hard stare. "Four years I was here and you never came to visit. Then you happen to find your divine vocation here? Perhaps when I invited you I should have said it was God calling."

Ryan glanced away awkwardly. "Come on Alma, that's not fair. We'd already grown apart before you came down here."

"If, by 'grown apart', you mean I refused to give up my own friends and interests just because you thought I was selling my soul to the devil."

Ryan sighed and offered a disarmingly handsome smile. "I was young and zealous, which can be a regrettable combination until life experience steps in and tempers one's outlook."

Alma set her gaze ahead and saw the same cafe from earlier coming up. "Does that mean you don't think I'm on a fast-track to hell anymore?"

"I would no longer dare to prescribe the fate of anyone's soul. That's God's business. I'm just one of the staff."

"So instead of writing judgement, you just frank the envelope. Not much of an improvement."

"I perform the sacraments and I guide people as best as I can. The difference now is that I've humility enough to see how ill-qualified I am."

"Sounds like the blind leading the blind. Doesn't the Bible say something about that?"

"It certainly does." Ryan laughed. "And it's as true today as ever it was. Can I get you a coffee?"

"I just had a coffee from here." Alma turned to face him, holding her bag in front of her. "I guess I've come full circle."

They said nothing for a moment, and she noticed another thing about him which had changed. As a teenager, he'd been terrible with eye contact. At least, he had been with her. Now, his gaze was confident and unwavering. She wondered if hearing the prayers and confessions of his flock had forced that awkwardness out of him.

Just as she felt a smile threatening to encroach on her lips, the door of the cafe opened and three young women stepped out. One of them with blonde hair looked aghast when she saw Alma.

"Oh my god, that's her," she said, nudging her nearest friend. "The screamer from the train."

The two other girls stared and giggled as they turned away, heading up towards the hill and the university campus. Alma lowered her face, her cheeks burning.

"What was that about?" Ryan asked delicately.

"It's nothing. I don't want to talk about it."

Ryan stooped to look her in the eye. *He really had changed.* "Do you still...get them? The dreams?"

"Don't call them dreams," Alma said, glowering. "I know what dreams feel like. Those were never dreams."

"*Were*? Or *are*? What happened on the train?"

Alma sucked in a breath and held it until she could decide what words, if any, to put on it.

"I must have fallen asleep. And, yes, it happened. That girl was sitting opposite me. I probably made her jump out of her skin."

"I'm sorry to hear that. That it's still happening to you, I mean. I didn't think you'd still be—"

"I haven't in months," Alma interrupted. "But a lot's happened recently. My brother's in trouble, I have to find a new place to live...it's just got my head in a spin. That's all it is."

Ryan nodded sympathetically all the time she spoke. Once again, she wondered if that was sincere or something he'd learned on the job.

"You don't have anywhere to live?" he asked.

"I had something, but it fell through. I'm sure I'll find something. It's a university town, there's always rooms to let."

"And always several thousand students looking to fill them. Especially right now. Can I help, at all?"

Alma tensed. "I couldn't ask you to...I couldn't impose..."

"Oh, I didn't mean invite you to stay with me. Given my position, that wouldn't be appropriate anyway."

"No, of course." Alma sagged, assuring herself that it was with relief.

"I'll ask around, though. I know quite a few people who let property in the town. Give me a couple of days and I might have some leads."

"That would be great," Alma said, forcing a weak smile. "Worst case, I'll find a B&B for a few nights."

Ryan plucked a business card from his breast pocket and handed it to her. Her face broke into a smirk when she read it.

"Father Ryan Bidgood. It doesn't suit you at all."

"I agree. If it helps, you can still just call me Ryan."

"It helps a little."

Ryan chuckled softly and Alma felt heat in her face again. She took out her phone to enter his number and noticed the time. "Ah crap. I'm meeting my new boss in half an hour."

"You'd better get going then," Ryan said. "It'll take you twenty minutes to walk up the hill."

"Actually, by my third year I could do it in about fifteen."

In the square across the road, a group of obvious students emerged from a pub, dragging their luggage over the cobbles towards the hill. Seeing them reminded her of the bag at her own feet. Fifteen minutes was probably optimistic. She slipped her phone and card into her pocket.

"Thanks for this, Ryan. I'll send you a text so you have my number. Anything really would be a help."

Ryan rubbed a hand on his cheek, as if blighted by a sudden unease.

"I'm sorry I used to be so judgemental," he said. "That's not to say I wouldn't prefer to see you choose a different path. But if you're willing to give me another chance, I'm ready to see a childhood friend in you again. Not just the girl who went off and got involved with witchcraft and stuff."

Alma shifted her weight and folded her arms. "I'm both of those people, Ryan. You realise that, don't you?"

"Yes, I know. And I'd love it if both of those people would meet me for a drink and a proper catch up one evening. Whenever you have time."

Alma studied his face and, for the first time that day, managed to see past the dog collar.

"I'd like that."

Chapter 3

Alma reached the top of the concrete steps, almost forgetting she was not part of the throng of students swarming to the right, towards the student union. The paved courtyard and the concrete buildings that lined it on three sides presented a landscape of grey-brown, save for two square wooden planters with benches, and a bold teal canopy with a sign that read 'Canolfan y Celfyddydau Aberystwyth Arts Centre'.

When she had first been here, it had been from attending sixth form in one of the most deprived parts of North Wales. The grimy brutalist structures of the library and arts centre had seemed practically space-age to her.

Now, having lived in the vibrant and fast-developing metropolis of Manchester for three years, the impact was quite different. Her life in the city felt a long way away, and even that was an optimistic assessment. In truth, her life in Manchester was over.

That sombre reminder propelled her across the forecourt and through the automatic glass doors of the arts centre. A cheerful woman with a volunteer badge pinned to her pastel purple shirt immediately sprang up from behind a desk.

"Hello there," the woman said, reaching for a cluster of prepared plastic bags. "Are you looking for the residence halls or the union?"

Alma approached the desk and set her bag and backpack on the floor, rolling the ache out of her shoulder. "Neither. I'm here to see Doctor Stacpoole. It's Alma Petrulytė."

27

"Oh right." The receptionist nodded and reached for her desk phone. "I'm not sure if he's in his office yet, I'll just…"

She was interrupted by a single sharp hand clap. Alma jolted. A man's voice followed.

"Don't worry about that, Kelly. I'm here."

Alma turned and saw a man with a round face with black hair in a messy comb over. He was wearing an Iron Maiden t-shirt and a black leather waistcoat with jeans. Despite his appearance, his confident grin and outstretched hand banished all doubt about who he must be.

"Doctor Stacpoole?" she asked, offering her hand in return.

"That's me," he said, taking it firmly and clasping his other hand over the top. "But let's do away with the 'doctor' nonsense. Call me Damien, or Stackers if you prefer. That's what everyone calls me."

"Alright," Alma said. "Damien. Good to meet you at last."

Damien looked her in the eye intensely. "*Malonu susipažinti.*"

"Very impressive," Alma said. "But I'm afraid I don't actually speak Lithuanian."

"Really? Your profile says you were born in Vilnius."

The question wrongfooted Alma, not least because she had not extended any social media invites to Dr Stacpoole.

"I was still a baby when my parents moved to the UK."

28

"That's a shame. I learned quite a bit for the occasion."
He slipped his hands into his jeans pockets, like a
peacock retracting its feathers.

Alma shrugged and gave him a thin-lipped smile.
"Sorry."

Damien led her through the ground floor, away from the
modern theatre foyer and down a corridor that reminded
her of school, with a concrete floor you could still hear
through the thin carpet and the dirty stippled panels of a
suspended ceiling. The door he stopped at had a sign
printed on blue card, laminated and fixed to the door with
drawing pins: 'Centre for Studies in the Visual Culture of
Religion'. It was a stark contrast to the other doors in the
corridor, which all had embossed name plaques.

"Have you not had a chance to get settled yet?" Damien
asked, nodding at her bags as he unlocked the door and
pushed it open.

"I just got off the train less than an hour ago. I'm afraid
it's all been a little bit— Oh!"

As soon as Alma walked through the door, she was
assailed by two scrambling paws and a wild-eyed smiling
maw. She didn't have a free arm to shield herself, so the
unexpected border collie pushed her back against the
wall.

"Flick! Down!" Damien grabbed the dog by its collar.
"Sorry about that. I should have warned you. Are you
alright with dogs?"

"I love dogs." Alma laughed breathily, composing
herself. She looked for somewhere to put her bags down,
but quickly realised that desk space was a scarce
commodity. The office was significantly longer than it
was wide, made even more so by a row of freestanding

metal shelves. A continuous desk ran down the side with two pairs of flat screen monitors, and a square wooden table with plastic chairs sat obstructively in the middle. The room had a stale, cardboardy smell.

"One of my roommates normally looks after her during the day," Damien said, ushering the dog towards a cushioned bed underneath the desk. "But neither of them are back until next week, so Flick will be joining us until then."

Alma perched on the edge of the table while Damien settled the dog and then started searching the desk for something. The office was by no means a comfortable space, but she was grateful to rest her legs after the walk up the hill.

"I'm afraid it'll just be a lot of reading to begin with," Damien said. "We're not in the most organised state. Your predecessor didn't leave under the best of terms."

"Oh dear." Alma hid a yawn. The continual walking might have been the only thing keeping tiredness at bay. Pushing away from the table, she knelt down to reach under the desk and stroke Flick's head. The dog panted happily.

Damien lifted keyboards and checked in between books that had been in place so long they had acquired a layer of dust, apparently not finding what he was looking for. As Alma petted the dog, she was aware of her new colleague's prolonged glances every time he seemed to think she wouldn't notice.

"I had some HR stuff for you to fill out," he said. "I'm sure I left it here. Maybe it's still at my house." He planted his fists on his hips and blew out a puff of air. "It's not far, actually. You could come back with me and

30

grab some lunch. Pick up the papers while we're there. It'll be more comfortable than the office."

Alma scrambled for a polite reason to decline the invitation, which she suspected had not been entirely spontaneous.

"That's alright, you don't have to feed me," she said, laughing it off. "Could you just print out the forms again?"

"Excellent." Damien nodded, turning slightly red. "I'll do that."

He woke up one of the computers, clicked a few times and then excused himself to go to the reprographics room. When he was gone, Alma hung her coat on the back of a chair and drifted to a bookshelf at the far end of the room. Ring-binders outnumbered actual books, most of them labelled as course material, but there were also textbooks and box files unrelated to Damien's work.

As she scanned the titles — wondering if it was possible Damien had invented a research centre and converted a stockroom into an office just so he could perform his 'the HR paperwork is back at my place' routine — she noticed an alcove in the back corner. She peered around, suddenly flinched, and then laughed, shaking her head in self-ridicule.

Hanging on the wall was a framed print of a drawing. The subject was a figure with a goat's head marked with a pentagram on a female human bust with feathered wings behind. Alma confronted it, arms folded, the musty office all but forgotten.

As she stared, the background of the picture came alive in her mind's eye. She saw the pale greys, pinks and blues of an Anglesea sunset, the heavy clouds carrying

31

rain in from the sea. The eyes of the goat stared back at her, as through a window. Rivulets of blood began to trickle down the human chest from underneath the goat's beard.

Alma's lips thinned. She remained facing the picture, but what she was seeing came more now from her mind than from her eyes. She conjured up the fear she had once felt, and clenched her fists. *She was not afraid anymore...*

"Are you two having a moment?" Damien's voice arrested her attention. "Should I come back later?"

Alma stepped away from the alcove. "No, it's OK. We're old friends."

"Of course, your PhD dissertation. *Fear and Realisation.* Goats seem to feature quite heavily in your analysis."

"I suppose you could call it a dread fascination." Alma shrugged. "I wanted to talk about how people embody their fears in art in order to have a physical manifestation they can square up to. In the past, goats evoked much more fear than they do today, albeit mostly because of superstition."

Damien cocked his head towards the picture with a raised brow. "I take it you are keeping capraphobia alive in the twenty first century. What is it? The Satanic connotations? The blank stare?"

"The humble goat gave the devil his horns," Alma explained. "Until he was conflated with the goat god, Pan, the devil was never depicted with horns. In Matthew's Gospel, we are told that on the day of judgement God will separate mankind like a shepherd separates the sheep from the goats. And the goats are the ones who are sent to eternal fire."

"Goats are the denizens of hell?" Demiel reeled back theatrically. "And to think I took my niece to feed them at the petting zoo."

Alma nodded gravely. "They were earmarking her soul for damnation the entire time, I promise you."

"Naturally. So that's why you have a fear of goats?

"Actually no." Alma felt the corner of her mouth quirk involuntarily. "It's much simpler than that. When I was five, my family stayed over with friends who lived on a farm. I went into a room I shouldn't have and came face to face with a slaughtered goat hung up to drain."

Damien winced and chuckled. "I bet that gave you nightmares for a while."

"You have no idea." Alma's smile faltered. Damien wasn't standing particularly close, but his gaze invaded her space. She glanced at the papers in his hand. "Shall I fill those out now?"

Damien accepted the digression and cleared a space for her to sit and write. Alma just about contained a gasp of alarm when her foot connected with something soft under the desk. The dog sprang up, tail wagging apologetically. Alma gave her a reassuring ruffle of the ears. Damien sat on the middle table and waited with his arms folded. The table creaked rhythmically with the swinging of his leg. Alma discreetly slid the form out of Damien's view as she skipped over the 'address' section.

She wasn't even onto the second page before Damien started asking questions like a bored child. Had Aberystwyth changed much since she'd been a student here? What sort of films was she into? Did she have any friends nearby? She answered blandly and unthinkingly,

and hoped none of her answers would invite a follow up.
It didn't work for long.

"Is Ryan someone you studied with?" The creaking of
the table had stopped, leaving the room uncomfortably
silent.

"No," Alma said, scratching harder with the pen to
replace the ambient noise. "An old friend from Anglesea.
I didn't know he lived here, actually. Just bumped into
him by chance this morning."

"That's nice. What does he do here?"

When Alma told him, Damien made a long 'ooh' sound
with an audible smile to it. Of course he was happy: a
Catholic priest could scarcely be a sexual rival.

With annoyance, she noticed her pen was hovering over
a question about her religion. She aggressively circled
'Rather not say' and continued with the form. Damien
continued the conversation largely by himself, describing
how he used to be part of the university debating society.
He related at length a particularly enjoyable occasion
when he'd roundly thrashed a Catholic apologist in a
public debate about Thomas Aquinas' Cosmological
Argument.

"I've just realised there's a problem," Alma said when
she couldn't take any more of his bragging. She picked
up the mostly-completed form and turned to see the face
of a man interrupted in his stride. "This is a little
embarrassing, but I don't actually have an address yet.
Can I give you that later?"

Damien's expression rallied. "No address? Where are
you staying?"

"I'm just trying to finalise something," Alma said,
wishing it wasn't an exaggeration. "There was some

confusion. Ryan's going to put me in touch with someone."

Damien hopped off the table and had his phone out of his pocket almost before his feet touched the floor. "Pfft, some oldiewonk from his church's parochial council probably. I think I might have something better for you."

"You know someone with a spare room?" Alma asked the question emphatically, hoping it would stop Damien's fingers mid-dial if this plan in any way involved her becoming his third roommate.

Damien held up a finger to excuse himself from responding until his call was answered. "Hey Robin, just a quick one. Are you still looking for someone to take that room? Awesome. I've got someone I think would be perfect." As he said that, he winked at Alma conspiratorially, though Alma wasn't sure what the secret was meant to be. "Are you gonna be home this evening? You're in all day! That's awesome. I'll give her your number and tell her to get in touch."

As he ended the call, Alma's mouth was open with nothing to say. Damien grinned at her and wrote something on a scrap of paper. He scribbled hurriedly, as though Alma might get a call from Ryan any moment with a better offer.

"Here you go." Damien thrust the note towards her. Alma noted with relief that the name of her prospective roommate was spelled with a 'y', and so presumably a girl's name. "She's my mate Jamie's ex. Used to live with us but she moved out when they broke up. We still get on OK. You'll like her. She's more our sort of people than whoever Ryan would have found you."

35

Setting aside Damien's assumption that she and him were in any way a 'kind of people', Alma smiled and slid the note into her pocket. "Thanks. That's a real help. I'll call her after we're done here."

Apparently that still allowed an unacceptable risk of Damien's plan being subverted by a counter offer from Ryan, because he started flapping his hands about and shaking his head.

"Don't worry about anything here," he said. "Like I said, it's mostly reading at first anyway. Why don't you take those forms and go see Robyn now?"

Alma asked if he was sure and he insisted he was. He would email her the links to their cloud drive, she should go get herself set up and they could pick up here tomorrow. Damien would be her knight in shining armour and, better still for him, would know where to find her.

But most importantly, as far as she was concerned, she didn't have to worry about paying for somewhere temporary to stay.

As Alma stood and gathered her bags, Flick jumped and wagged her tail, worrying that someone was about to leave.

"Thanks again Damien," Alma said. "I promise I'll be more organised tomorrow."

"Not a problem." Damien folded his arms high on his chest and nodded like a king bestowing a title. "I'm looking forward to working with you."

Alma smiled thinly and reached for the door. "Thanks. Me too."

The hill was hardly easier going down than going up. Alma took it slow and tried to be grateful that the rain clouds forming over the sea hadn't already arrived to make the walk even more treacherous. It was two in the afternoon and she had eaten nothing all day. Even the weakness in her arms and the rumbling of her stomach gave her no regrets for not taking lunch at Damien's house. True, if the room with Robyn worked out, then she owed Damien a big favour, but at least *this* wasn't something his imagination could interpret as a 'date'.

By the time she reached the town centre, Alma had phoned Robyn's number twice and been met with a busy tone both times, so she'd sent a text message. The address Damien had given was near the harbour. Alma wasn't prepared to go there until she'd made contact, or at least shaken off the unease which had trailed after her since she left the Arts Centre.

The route down the hill was so familiar that her focus turned inward rather than ahead. As it did, she saw the Sabbatic Goat from Damien's wall scowling at her, pentagram etched on its forehead and horns spread wide. With the image came the irrational sense that she had provoked it and now it was following her.

She stopped at a bus shelter, pretending to read the timetable as she lifted a hand to check her throat. There was nothing there, of course, but confirming it by touch was quicker than trying to reason with her own paranoia. Her fingers slid down to clasp the cluster of pendants. *I am here, I am now, and I can make peace with this moment.* Two more times she whispered the words, thumbing each pendant in turn. When she continued walking, her gaze was tethered to the clock tower in the

37

square up ahead. When she reached it, the sense of being watched had not abated and Robyn had not replied. Alma needed to find somewhere else to hide for a while.

Chapter 4

Scapegoat sat on the ancient stones, his fingers spread on a worn leather-bound volume in his lap, staring out at the town. He waited invisibly, as he had done for so long. Forgotten, like the crumbling walls around him.

As expected, she appeared on the seafront. He knew just where she was going, but he would not go to her now. He would not follow her. He would wait. She was walking the path he'd set her on when she was only a child. A path that would lead her to him.

So he watched from afar, the wind roaring righteously in his ears. Before long, she would call on him. Then she would know where the path lead.

The Arcana shop wasn't on the way, but the end of the seafront made an easy switchback to the harbour if Robyn messaged or called. The sign on the door had been flipped to 'Open', so Alma felt less like a trespasser this time as the bell jangled over her head. It was hardly better lit than it had been in the morning. The ambered wood smell was fresh from burning incense and a man with long salted black hair, bloated cheeks and messy stubble was leaning on the glass display counter reading a martial arts magazine.

"Y'right," he said with a fleeting glance.

Alma smiled. "You are open, yes?"

"Yeah, we're open," he said with a rolling Welsh accent. "Why do you ask?"

"Just that I came in this morning. The door was open, but the sign said closed, so I wasn't sure…"

The man cursed through his teeth and leaned towards the opening to the back of the shop. "Sara! You've bloody done it again! Sara? You there?"

When no reply came, the man tutted loudly and shook his head at Alma. "Told 'er enough times. How hard it is to pull a door shut properly? Anyway, come on in. We weren't open this morning, but we are now."

Alma considered putting a word in Sara's defence, pointing out that the wood of the door was old, swollen and probably unfit for purpose. She decided against it and put her bags down near the front, where they wouldn't risk knocking anything over in the confined space as she browsed.

Grateful for the silence as the man returned to his reading, she made her way around the chaotic displays. She therapeutically ran her fingers over leather journals, opened carved trinket boxes, and inspected amber jewellery for the prehistoric debris inside. Her hands-on perusing elicited no complaint from the owner, who was evidently as content not to be distracted from his reading as Alma was not to be asked if she was looking for anything in particular.

When she reached the display counter, she wondered if examining the contents was worth the disruption of asking the owner to slide his magazine out of the way. She lingered next to a rotating stand loaded with wooden beaded wristbands; it was close enough to the counter for her to observe without instigating an interaction with the shop owner. The counter contained an assortment of Wiccan ritual items: chalices, cauldrons, wands, altar candles, icons. Her interest was stoked by a row of ornate daggers, which was unfortunately hidden underneath the magazine and the elbows of its reader.

She inched closer and stooped to look at them until the man couldn't help but notice. He closed the magazine with a huff and stepped back. Alma mouthed a silent 'thank you' and stood up.

"Those are called *athames*," the man said. "They're just decorative, not actually for cutting. They're for focusing power during spells and rituals."

Alma politely pretended not to know that already, and nodded along as he told her how witches used them to carve symbols into candles. Her eyes were set on one particular dagger with a straight, roughly hammered blade and a small white and black goat's foot for a handle.

"They're very cool," she said and tapped the glass. "How much is that one?"

The man shuffled so that he was directly in front of Alma and could tell which one she was pointing at. When that didn't quite work, she helped him out by identifying it as 'the goat one'.

"You like that one, do you? It's quite unusual, very old too. An antique as it happens. Don't think anyone's ever asked about it before."

Alma nodded slowly, wondering if the man thought he'd answered her question. "Oh, sorry, is it not for sale then?"

The man pursed his lips and tilted his head one way then the other. "I'd sell it for eighty if you really like it."

It was more than Alma had expected. Certainly more than the small amount of cash she'd fled Manchester with. But she hadn't seen an athame like it before and she didn't feel up to haggling. "Yes, alright. I don't have enough right now, though. I guess it'll still be here at the end of the month."

"Tell you what, *cariad*," the man said, reaching up onto a shelf to get a key. "If you can give us a tenner now, I'll put it on layaway for you. You can pay for it in bits. How does that sound?"

Alma told him it sounded fine. She paid him ten pounds, and he took the goat-foot-handled dagger out of the cabinet and put it in a shallow box beneath the display. He made a point of showing Alma where he'd put it, "in case it's someone else in the shop next time".

With that done, she decided she'd probably been in the store long enough and went to collect her bags. Stepping towards the door, she noticed a flyer stuck on the glass which, unlike the many others, faced into the shop. It was a black and white photocopy of a hand-drawn poster for the 'Aberystwyth Wiccan Society'. Alma paused, impressed by the intricate symbols drawn around the edge of the poster, including some which were quite unusual and esoteric. It was quite unlike the clip-art riddled society posters she'd seen elsewhere around town. She read it twice, the first time thinking she must have missed the contact information, the second time realising there was none. Just a meeting time and an address.

"Do you know anything about this group?" She turned and saw the man hunched over his magazine, like an animatronic character returning to the origin of its sequence. He looked up with the same disinterested squint as when she'd come in.

"What now?" He peered and then huffed. "Never seen it before. Someone must've put it up without asking. Cheeky sods."

"Do you mind if I take it?"

"Help yourself. I'd only be taking it down anyway."

Alma folded the poster into her jacket pocket before stepping out onto the uncomfortably bright seafront road. She took out her phone, not that it was likely to have gone off in the shop without her hearing, but more to give her something to look at while her eyes adjusted to the daylight.

A pang of hunger came on in earnest. She suddenly remembered that what little money she had needed to last her until her first payday. Handing over ten pounds of it as a deposit for a ceremonial knife probably hadn't been the cleverest thing she'd done that day. Somehow, she still didn't regret it.

The phone rang in her hand with an unrecognised number. *About time.* Alma was quite done dragging the heavy bag around and had already decided it would take a real horror story for her to decline Robyn's spare room. For now, at least. Answering with a cheerful greeting that she hoped made her sound like the sort of person anyone would want as a roommate, she was unprepared for the furious bark that erupted from her phone's speaker.

"Where the fuck are you, you little bitch?"

Ice crystals exploded in Alma's veins. The edge of her vision throbbed in dark colours and the ground seemed to tilt. She dropped her bag, cursing that she hadn't thought to check the number on the screen was the same number on her scrap of paper.

"Filip…" Her words were thin, like half her voice was bleeding out through a wound in her throat. "…leave me alone. Please. I had to go. I can't help you anymore."

"*Maža kalė! I'm your brother! You don't just fucking run and hide when your family needs you.*"

That was one Lithuanian expression Alma was familiar with. *Maža kalė. Little whore.*

"You don't need me, Filip." Alma gripped the phone tightly, trying to force some strength back into her voice. "You need help. Real help. You have to turn yourself in."

"*You'd love that, wouldn't you? Ungrateful bitch. I always took care of you, Alma. And now you leave me outside for the fucking wolves?*"

"Don't blame me! I didn't put all this on your head. You did this to yourself."

"*Stop kidding yourself, Alma. You know the evil you brought into our lives. This is your fault. I protected you from it for years. Now it's your turn to do something for me.*"

Alma reached up to her neck, clutched her amulets and persuaded herself that he was lying. That he was wrong. She looked towards the rising cliff, the castle ruins, and the road dog-legging around towards the harbour.

"No, Filip. I'm sorry," she said, grabbing her bag and setting off at pace. "I will pray for you. But I'm not telling you where I am."

There was a moment of silence. When the voice returned, it was robed in an eerie calm.

"*Save your prayers, dear sister. You don't need to tell me anything. You can't hide from your big brother. I know where you are.*"

"Liar. You don't know anything." Alma quickened as she neared the bend. Gulls cried overhead. She was desperate to get away from any sound that could give Filip a clue.

"*I know you better than anyone. In fact, I can see you right now.*"

Alma's mouth gaped, silent and breathless. She looked behind her, down the promenade, then up the hill. Surely it wasn't possible. Surely he was just fucking with her mind. She hurried around the corner, throwing frantic glances over her shoulder.

A blistering screech filled her ears. Alma cried out and flinched, bringing her arms up defensively. Her bag fell and the phone jumped out of her hand, hitting the pavement with a sharp crack.

A weighty fog of malicious laughter descended on her. A group of five students, clapping their hands and cackling triumphantly. The closest one — the one who had screamed — was a young woman with short blonde hair. The girl from the train.

"See how you like it, freak!" the blonde said, turning and leading the group away. Their hooting and sneering faded down a street leading back into town.

Alma was frozen and unable to speak. Her shoulders heaved as she battled to control her breathing. She waited until her arms no longer felt encased in cement, then searched for her phone. The words 'Call ended' lay behind a prominent crack in the screen.

45

The road ahead was empty, yet Alma felt a thousand eyes watching her from every angle. She switched her phone off and buried it deep in her jacket pocket. The prospect of answering it again now held more anxiety than the notion of turning up at a stranger's house asking for a place to live.

Willing her legs into motion, she selected an object to anchor her gaze to until she reached it. Then she picked another, and another, until the last one she picked was a sign with the name of the road Damien had written down.

Chapter 5

Alma found the house number screwed into an unpainted wooden gate in a stone wall next to a tattoo parlour. Over the wall was the rear of a house that stood out from the others in the terrace. The white paint was many years overdue for a fresh coat, and the irregular brickwork gave it a texture like old dried bandages. The mummified house had diamond leaded windows in brown wooden frames. One window had a vivid purple roller blind pulled down, the others were dark.

Alma went through the unlatched gate and battled with her bags up some creaking wooden steps to the first-floor flat. It was within a glass-walled porch with a mint-green and honey coloured frame that looked borrowed from a nicer house.

She knocked on the door briskly, hoping the exertion of the steps would counteract the pale fright that lingered on her face. While she waited for an answer, she slipped a hand into her jacket pocket, ready to show her blank, shattered phone if asked why she hadn't answered a recent call.

The creaking of floorboards was audible even through the door. When it opened, a heady waft of sandalwood incense and microwave meals immediately invited Alma to call this place home. The door opened to the length of the security chain, and a woman close to Alma's age peered through. She had downturned eyes and purple hair hanging off her shoulder that matched the colour of the bedroom blind.

"Oh, you're here!" she said, turning slightly red. She released the chain and opening the door fully, revealing a curvy form in a tank top and baggy jeans. "Alma, is it? I'm Robyn. Come in. Damien didn't say when to expect you."

Alma hauled her bags for what she hoped was the last time that day and followed into a dingy entrance lobby with seven laminated pine doors. It seemed like more doors than the flat could possibly have rooms.

"I know," she said. "Damien didn't say much about anything to me, either. Just your address and phone number. I did try calling ahead."

Robyn sucked in her lips and nodded sheepishly. "Sorry about that. I was on the phone to Damien again, actually. He really wants me to get you to move in. Told me lots about you." She smiled and added the obligatory, "All good things."

"I'm glad to hear it, considering I only met him for the first time this morning."

Two of the doors were already open. One led to a brown and blue kitchen, if 'kitchen' was what you called a place where frying pans went to die after becoming too caked in burnt grease. The other opened into a surprisingly large sitting room, made smaller by dark blue wallpaper with gold stars and moons, shelving units brimming with trinkets and cartoon collectibles, and a sofa hidden under a purple throw.

Robyn opened another door and invited Alma to go first. "You obviously made a good first impression. Not surprising. You're very much his type."

Alma felt the first pang of hesitation. "His words? Or yours?"

Robyn studied her reaction and broke into a wide, warm smile.

48

"Don't worry," she said. "Damien likes to think of himself as a bit of a rock star, but he's harmless. Lovely guy, really. He didn't say anything like that about you. Just that you are interesting and nice and that he thought you'd be a good fit."

"Well, I hope that's true. About being a good fit, I mean." Alma committed herself over the threshold of the room. It was small and had orange walls, a single bed, a pine-laminated bedside table and just about enough remaining floor space for her luggage.

Alma piled her two bags at the foot of the bed and stretched her arms in front of her, revelling in unburdened bliss. She looked out the diamond-leaded window which overlooked the tiny yard and the back of the tattoo shop. The main street was out of view.

Nothing could see her. A perfect hiding place.

Robyn left her to decide about the room without the pressure of someone lingering. As soon as she was alone, Alma could feel the resonance of fear in her hands. A plastic curtain track hung over the window, but no curtains. She took off her jacket and emptied the record of her day from her pockets: three creased train tickets - Manchester Piccadilly to Crewe, then to Shrewsbury, then to Aberystwyth - Ryan's contact card, Damien's note, the flyer from the Arcana shop and her phone.

Daubing her fingers gently on the cracked screen, she wrote a message to Ryan letting him know that she'd found somewhere to stay, and that she'd be in touch about going for a drink. She sent the second draft of the message; the first draft had asked if he was available for a drink tonight.

The conversation looked so strange on her phone after she saved his name. Ryan Bidgood and a conversation with just one message. She remembered a time long ago when his name sat above a text conversation that went back endlessly. If she still had the phone she'd owned then, she knew she could scroll up and see dozens of messages each day, sometimes amounting to nothing more than telling each other how bored they were. Other times, they were grand plans that may or may not have ever come to fruition.

Towards the end, they were littered with Ryan's efforts to make church groups and events sound appealing, greased in transparent flattery that Alma was better than the life she'd chosen. His messages had become longer, while hers had become shorter.

Alma wondered what the last messages between them had been. Those conversations, however much they had changed over time, were never deleted, just presumed to have died with that old phone. She re-read the message she'd just sent. A new conversation, beginning behind a newly cracked screen.

"Everything OK?"

Alma turned to see Robyn in the doorway, looking concerned. She must have not heard her speak. "Sure...sorry, did you say something?"

"I just asked if you wanted a cup of tea or coffee."

"No, thanks. Maybe just some water."

"No problem," Robyn said, studying Alma's face. "I hope the room's big enough. I'm sure Damien told you nothing about what you were walking into."

"It's fine, honestly. I really appreciate this. I had no idea what else I was going to do."

50

Alma followed Robyn into the lounge and took a place on the sofa. The purple throw was saturated with the fragrance of late evenings, of incense and weed and hours of TV bingeing. It was calming to imagine her own eventual inclusion in the olfactory montage.

"Damien said you just came from Manchester." Robyn set a glass of water on top of a steamer trunk, which served as a coffee table. "You move down because of the job?"

"Mm, yes. Well, mostly that."

Breathing took a lot of concentration and left little with which to form words. The window in this room had thin beige curtains pulled across it. Alma thought it probably faced the road. Robyn sat down beside her.

"You sure you're OK?" Robyn turned to face her, cross-legged and too close, but Alma forced a smile and tried not to inch away.

"I'm sure. It's just been a busy day. Busy and a little weird. Sorry, I'm not normally like this, I promise."

"Don't apologise. Damien didn't freak you out too much this morning, did he? He can take some getting used to."

"No, it's not that at all. It's a whole load of stuff. I don't want to offload the second I meet you. I'm supposed to be making you *want* to let me move in."

Robyn hummed thoughtfully, then reached down to the side of the steamer trunk and pulled open a hidden draw. She took out a wooden grinder pot with a brass pentagram inlay, a pack of tobacco, some rolling papers and a ziplock bag of weed.

"Fair enough," she said. "In that case, let's become friends. Then you can offload and make yourself at home. You smoke?"

She held up the clear bag and gave it a shake. Alma felt the tension in her chest loosen and she let it escape as laughter.

"Today, absolutely."

It was always the same in the first week of a new term: the new students in the residential halls kept their doors closed. They all wanted to enjoy being the rulers of their own little new world before they would entertain the idea of socialising. Of meeting other people.

Of looking out for the wellbeing of their neighbours.

Music played behind door twenty-six, but not as loud as the music behind door twenty-four. This year, the university welcome pack had included a small 'magic drawing pad': the kind you wrote on with a plastic stylus and then moved a slider at the bottom to erase your work. Many of the new students had tacked their pad onto the outside of their doors. The one on room twenty-six had the name 'Claire' written on it, framed by little hearts.

Scapegoat knocked firmly, then stepped back. When the door opened, a gush of tinny reggaeton music and newfound independence spilled out. A short-haired blonde presented herself like a movie star emerging from a dressing room, but her smile quickly dropped. No doubt she hadn't expected to have dealings with an older adult until lectures began.

"Oh hello," Scapegoat said, lifting the ID badge on a university lanyard. "Claire Warwick? Do I have the right room?"

"Yes." The girl spoke indignantly and impatiently, eyeing the badge as a solitary concession to his right to be there.

"Sorry to be a bother. There's someone from the police in reception wanting to talk to you about somebody you might have seen on the train this morning."

Claire folded her arms in front of her. "The police? Am I in trouble?"

"I'm sure you're not. It sounds like they just want to know if you might have seen something. They wanted to come to your room and ask, but I thought you might prefer if I came and got you. No need to make a big fuss on everyone's first day."

"Oh, I see," Claire said, chewing her lip at the suggestion she might have spent the rest of the year known as the girl who had a visit from the police on her first day. "Yes, thank you. There was somebody strange on the train, but I didn't really see them do anything. I don't know how much I can tell them."

Scapegoat lifted his shoulders exaggeratedly and held his hands out to the side. "I wouldn't worry. I'm sure they're probably covering all bases. Come on, let's get it over with and you'll be back here in no time."

He didn't wait for her answer before striking off down the corridor towards the stairwell lobby. Ahead of him on the left, a door opened and a greasy face peered out, then retracted immediately upon seeing him. The varieties of music behind the different doors merged like a jungle chorus.

Scapegoat paused in the lobby and looked back to see Claire hurrying after him, trying to fit a very large phone into the small pocket of her skinny jeans. She hadn't put on a jacket; she believed him that this wouldn't take long. She was only too eager to believe it.

Outside, he indicated his car, parked on the grass verge in front of the residence halls. Groups of students were coming and going, all of them far too consumed with their elevation to adulthood to notice him, his car, or the ashen-faced blonde. Scapegoat glanced back at her and winked, tacitly assuring her that nobody would remember seeing the two of them together.

Chapter 6

A veil of smoke patrolled around the sofa, shrouding them from the world outside. Alma felt no unease about the detail in which she'd related the story of her morning to Robyn. Part way through, Robyn even seemed to notice that Alma hadn't mentioned stopping to eat, and so had left unbid to put a pizza in the oven. Alma was past feeling hungry, but the smell of crusty dough and cheese soon had her mouth watering.

Only when she got to the last episode of her day did she decide it was better to skimp on detail.

"And then, to top it off, my brother phoned me and started biting my head off about leaving without telling him. I'd been deflecting his calls all morning, but he used a different phone and I thought it was you. Then, while I'm talking to him, the girl from the train comes along and jump-scares the shit out of me to get her own back and...well, this is the pièce de résistance."

Alma took out her cracked phone and held it screen-side-out. Robyn nodded and grimaced, though her eyes were already wide with hunger for more of the story.

"You know what I'm going to ask next, don't you?" she said. "Why didn't you tell your brother you were coming to Aber?"

"That's a really tedious story," Alma sighed. She needed to keep Filip outside the ring of protection formed by the smoke and the smells for a while longer.

Robyn's curiosity could not be halted. So when she went to collect the food, Alma had to decide where it could be redirected. Though she stood slowly, her body still took a moment to catch up with her head. She scanned a shelf of DVDs: mostly classic eighties action movies, supernatural drama series and lots of anime. There were boxes, vials, goblets, and pouches styled with runes and pagan symbols. Probably more than even Alma had ever owned. The ritual items would have made a productive talking point if they weren't obviously for display rather than use. In fact, they served mostly to punctuate a dense throng of vinyl figurines and plastic "Bad Taste Bears" statues.

When the pizza came out — with a bowl of chunky chips and the largest bottle of ketchup she'd ever seen — Alma told Robyn about working at the John Ryland Library archives for the two years after finishing her PhD, and about how she had lived in Wales since before she could walk and had been the only non-bilingual member of her Lithuanian family until she started learning Welsh at school.

In turn, Alma learned Robyn was a Radiology Technician at Bronglais Hospital, meaning that she had less of a walk up the hill to work than Alma did. Robyn professed herself as a film and anime nut but not much of a cook, even though those things were readily evident.

With a full stomach and a light head, Alma found the conversation flowing without the need for any great substance, until Robyn clicked her fingers and sat bolt upright.

"So...the goat thing?"

Alma shook her head with a confused hum and a shake of her head, before realising that Damien must have made her admission in his office sound much more interesting than it really was. Robyn explained that he'd sold a narrative where Alma had seen a dead goat as a child and was now deathly afraid of them. She even confessed to having taken down a band poster with a Baphomet sigil on it before Alma arrived.

"You needn't have worried." Alma forced a laugh, glancing about for a bare space on the wall where the poster might have been. "Damien read my PhD dissertation on fear and imagery. If he thinks it was just about my childhood fear of goats, then I suppose that doesn't say much for my thesis."

"So go on then, give me the fly-by of your theories about 'fear and imagery'."

Alma has seldom met anyone interested enough to ask her to explain it in simple terms, which reminded her how difficult it had been to do the opposite — make it complex enough to fill a hundred pages for her doctorate.

"Let me start with a question," she said. "What's the famous literary work depicting the afterlife written by Dante Alighieri?"

Robyn snapped her fingers and answered without hesitation. "*Inferno*. Virgil going through the nine circles of hell."

"That's the answer almost everyone gives. Few remember that Inferno was one part of a bigger work: *The Divine Comedy*. So although *Inferno* isn't strictly incorrect, it's particularly interesting that nobody ever just names *Purgatorio* or *Paradiso*."

Robyn took a slow drag of the joint and nodded thoughtfully. "I guess people find hell more interesting."

"Exactly. Because the imagery in *Inferno* was cautionary, imparting fear. When it comes to both literature and imagery, studies have shown that fear cues prompt in humans a state of defensive motivation in which autonomic and somatic survival reflexes are enhanced."

Robyn squinted at her. "I think I might be more stoned than you are. Come again?"

Alma smiled. "In other words, being presented with images of safety and fulfilment dull our senses, whereas being presented with our fears heightens them. It gives us an experience that is both compelling and memorable."

"Is that why so much of Damien's religious art is of people being punished by demons in a lake of fire rather than playing harps on clouds?"

"Essentially, yes. Skulls and other symbols of death were common in mediaeval churches to remind the faithful that one day they would die and face judgement. And in a time when people universally believed in an afterlife, images of eternal torment were a far more effective call to action than the promise of paradise."

"So we should put up more pictures of things that frighten us to keep us motivated, is that the gist of it?"

"Not quite. You're more likely to experience it today in the media. Scaremongering headlines to sell newspapers. Depictions of little green monsters in between your teeth to sell toothpaste."

Robyn hummed and passed the joint to Alma. "So how did seeing a dead goat as a child lead you to write a PhD on scary art?"

"It wasn't just about seeing a dead goat. I know it was just an animal that had been butchered and hung up for the blood to drain."

Robyn leaned forward, holding a slice of pizza with cheese dangerously close to sliding off onto the sofa. "But clearly it made a lasting impression."

Alma sighed and looked over to the window. "My family were staying at a friend's farmhouse. I was six at the time. My brother was twelve, the same age as the son who lived there. As a joke, they told me that dad wanted to see me in one of the outbuildings. They knew what I would find in there."

"That's a nasty prank to pull on a six-year-old. But it's no great mystery: young boys are shits."

Alma chuckled grimly. "That's not all, though. I shut myself in my room. My parents tried to comfort me, but I wouldn't come out, not even for dinner."

"Maybe you should have. If the goat was for dinner, you could have eaten the source of your fear." Robyn grinned an inebriated grin, then devoured the pizza slice just in time to save the purple throw from being cheesed.

"Maybe. That evening, I couldn't sleep. I heard something outside and, when I looked, I saw the head of the goat right there in the window."

"Oh, shit!" Robyn put a fist to her mouth. "That's grim. I bet the boys got a right bollocking for that, didn't they?"

"One of them did," Alma said. She took a drag and blew smoke to reinforce the hazy perimeter, then passed it back to Robyn. "My brother was in the attic room at the time, so it's unlikely he could have done it without being seen. The other boy insisted he had nothing to do with it. But when my parents found me in bed screaming and bawling, the goat's head was gone. So who knows what really happened."

Robyn tapped the joint against her lips and peered at Alma like she was trying to figure out a riddle.

"Well, it must have been one of them, right?"

"I don't know." Alma shrugged. "Things changed a lot after that day. My parent's relationship became acrimonious to say the least. My brother became angry and violent and started getting into trouble with the police. At school, three of my closest friends died: two in car accidents and one in a house fire. Filip told me that it was the devil I'd seen in my window that night, and that there was a curse on me. He said the only way I could be protected from evil was to be loyal to him. To do whatever he told me."

Robyn's jaw fell. "What...sort of things did he tell you to do? You don't mean...like..."

"No, nothing like that." Alma shook her head earnestly. "But it frequently meant lying for him. Covering for him. Taking the blame for things he'd done. No punishment from our parents scared me more than the evil Filip said was out to get me."

"That's sick. You got wise though, right? When did you finally realise he was playing you?"

Alma looked away, unable to answer. Her hand closed around her pendants, the metal edges digging into her palm. A moment passed, and she felt Robyn's hand on her knee.

"You *do* know he was manipulating you, don't you?"

"Of course," Alma said. "But I also know that all the worst things that happened growing up happened when I refused to do what Filip said. And those were the times..."

Alma stopped herself, remembering that Robyn was someone who was offering her a place to live. Nobody offered their spare room to someone who believed they

60

were cursed. Or who had seen goats' heads in their window almost nightly for most of their life.

"Does your brother still think he's protecting you?"

"I don't know what he thinks. He went off the rails after he left school, and I learned to take care of myself. That's the point I make in my thesis, actually, about the realisation of fear through imagery. When you intentionally look at a depiction of something that scares you, the fear cue becomes consciously self-administered and is therefore not just motivation, but empowerment. You contain your fear in one place. It's no longer in the shadows. It is somewhere you can see it."

Robyn scratched at the corner of her mouth. "The only thing that frightens me is the idea of someone else thinking they need to protect me. That's what it was like with my ex. He believed in old-school chivalry. At least that's what he called it. What it really meant was that any time I proved capable of looking after myself, he felt emasculated."

"Sounds a lot like my brother. Hating the idea of you having any power or strength of your own?"

"Right!" Robyn became cartoonishly animated. "Fuck that. I have my own power, and anyone who doesn't like it can shove it up their arse."

Alma lifted her gaze to the shelf with the ritual paraphernalia. "Out of interest, did you ever take your power from any of that stuff?"

Robyn was comfortably positioned with her legs crossed, and tried a couple of times to turn and see what Alma was talking about without moving too much.

"What, you mean, like witchcraft and all that? There used to be a few of us who tried some spells, but it was just a bit of fun, really. The others lost interest really quickly."

"That's a shame. I had a group of friends I explored pagan mysticism with for a long time. While I was studying here, actually."

Robyn threw her a wide-eyed grin. "You're kidding? Please tell me you're a *bona fide* witch. That would be the coolest thing."

"I don't know about that. But we tried out different forms of magic. Researched ways to seek the blessing of different gods and goddesses. I mean, honestly, it was mostly a social thing but..." Alma's face and shoulders relaxed, and she realised she was smiling. "...it made me feel safe for a long time."

"Which your brother resented, I bet."

"Yeah, that's true. But he had troubles of his own by then. I even cast a few rituals to help him, but no god or goddess can help a person who won't help themselves."

"Amen." Robyn clapped her hands. "Or wait, no, that's a Christian thing, isn't it? What is it that pagans say?"

"'Amen' is fine. It just means 'so be it' in Hebrew. But a lot of people use an old English equivalent: 'so mote it be'."

"*So mote it be*. Awesome. We should start up a coven of our own. You can teach me the ways."

Alma laughed at the idea, fairly certain it wasn't the sort of commitment Robyn would make so haphazardly if she wasn't stoned. She rested her head on her arm and tried to think of a simple ritual they could do with what was on the shelf. If nothing else, it could entertain and cement Alma's claim as the new flatmate.

Then she remembered the flyer in her room. She'd meant to ask Robyn if she'd ever been into the Arcana shop, though the contents of her shelves made it impossible to believe she hadn't at some point.

"I did check to see if there were any communities in the area," Alma said. "It didn't look like there were until I saw this."

She hopped up and retrieved the flyer from her room. Robyn squinted at it when it was handed to her.

"Aberystwyth Wiccan Society? How have I never heard of this?"

"Perhaps they're new."

"Freshers, you think?"

Alma shrugged. "I don't know. It doesn't have a student-y feel about it."

"Well," Robyn said, pushing herself up. "There's only one way to find out. Let's get ourselves down there. Come on, they're meeting tonight. It can be our first time going out together as flatmates."

It felt as much a dare as an invitation. Alma had expected to spend this first evening being introduced to some niche animated series, probably falling asleep right where she was sat. Smoke some more. Delay the difficult conversation about what Alma could actually afford to put down as a deposit.

Instead, there was a jangling of keys from the hall and Robyn was in the doorway with her jacket on.

"You're really serious about doing this?" Alma asked, tentatively rising from the sofa.

"Hell yes. I'm doing this, even if you're not. But there's less chance of me making a tit of myself if you come."

63

Alma was in no position to refuse. Robyn hadn't asked for a penny so far. Instead, she was asking for a guide into a world Alma knew well. Assuming, of course, that the 'Aberystwyth Wiccan Society' wasn't just a bunch of drama students doing some live action roleplay of the witches scene from Macbeth.

No. The flyer was more promising than that. And for the first time since she'd arrived in town, Alma saw an opportunity to hit back against the spectre that had been following her around all day.

"I'll get my coat."

Chapter 7

The flyer directed them to an end-terrace house in a small estate part way up the hill. It distinguished itself from the other houses on the street by its broken and boarded windows, and the wildly overgrown hedge clambering up in front. If it weren't for a dim glow behind the wired glass of the front door, Alma would have assumed it was derelict.

"Not students then," Robyn said. She was right: no chance anyone would get away with renting out a place in that condition.

Alma looked at the flyer and then the plastic numbers on the green wooden door, hoping they'd made a mistake. When she looked at the adjacent house, she saw a brand new seven-seater Audi. In the lit kitchen window, a well-presented middle-aged woman was washing dishes. The contrast was stark.

"It's definitely the place."

"You think we should knock?"

"Might as well," Alma said, keeping the flyer in her hand in case someone demanded to see why she was at their house. "If it was a house in the woods looking like that, I'd probably say no."

"Agreed. If someone attacks us with a chainsaw, the neighbours at least look like they'd come and complain about the noise."

"Excellent. We're really thinking this through like adults."

Alma walked up to the front door and rapped it hard. The glow inside the ramshackle house intensified: a door opening within. A lanky silhouette materialised behind

65

the front door window just before it opened and a man spoke.

"Have you come for the meeting?"

Alma's immediate thought was that she'd never heard such a heavy Welsh accent from a man who looked so much like Bob Marley, complete with dreadlocks and beads in his goatee. Without the softening effect of the wired glass, he was less willowy and much leaner than he'd first seemed.

"This meeting, yes?" She held up the flyer. The man simply turned around and ambled down the hall, gesturing for them to follow. Alma hesitated at the door. "We're not late are we?"

"Not at all." The man stood in the doorways to the only lit room. A flickering light, not electrical. "Come in. Make yourselves comfortable. My name's Gerallt."

Curiosity drew Alma in first, and she followed Gerallt into a candlelit room with dirty yellow walls and a brown and orange patterned carpet. A scattering of mismatched cushions and blankets provided the only furnishing. The window was covered with a large plywood panel nailed in place. The ceiling light fitting had no bulb. Instead, half a dozen pillar candles were arranged on a brown-tiled hearth beneath an unlit gas fire. The only warmth came from a small camping stove, atop which was a black pot, and several wooden trinket boxes sat beside it.

As they entered, Alma glanced at Robyn and silently mouthed, *'Are you OK with this?'* Robyn shrugged and nodded. Alma wrinkled her nose and mimed laughter: one way or another, this was going to be interesting.

Gerallt sat cross-legged on the floor behind the gas stove and gestured for the two women to sit opposite.

Alma kept her bag slung across her body, reaching down to check that the carpet was actually dry. She set herself down and leaned forward to look into the pot. It was filled with pitted dark grey pebbles and radiated a welcome warmth.

"How many people normally come to these meetings?" she asked.

"Sometimes lots, sometimes none. Tonight, I'm only expecting you two."

"Oh, you were expecting us?" Alma discreetly caught Robyn's eye. "Was that some kind of foresight?"

"Nothing like that at all. I expect that people who have a reason will come. You came. You had a reason. It is just as I expected."

"That's profound." Robyn smirked. "So just to clarify, you're not expecting anyone else? No regulars?"

Gerallt didn't reply. Instead, he crossed his long arms in front of him and pulled his t-shirt up over his head slowly. Alma had plenty of time to regard his well-toned body, and the wizened face of the Celtic 'Green Man' tattoo scowling from his chest. She hastened to strike all evidence of interest from her face as Gerallt tossed the shirt aside and extended a hand towards her.

"I prefer to lay myself bare to the spirits," he said. "You two are invited to do the same if you wish."

A laugh burst from Alma's mouth. She cocked her head at him. "I'm going to need to be a *lot* more impressed before I start taking any clothes off."

"Your choice." Gerallt smiled and opened one of the boxes beside the stove. He took out three tiny twisted parcels, like miniature wonton dumplings made from something yellow-green and leathery. He popped one into his mouth and chewed while offering the other two to Alma and Robyn.

Alma took the ball and gave it a sniff. It was pungent with a fragrance she couldn't place.

"Just chew?"

"Correct. And don't swallow," Gerallt said. His eyes were narrowed, and green flecks showed between his teeth as he spoke.

She considered the strange herb, wondering if she should be encouraged by the fact that their host had readily led by example. She noticed in her periphery that Robyn was watching, waiting for her to go first.

Curiosity prevailed. Alma placed it into the side of her mouth and crushed it between her teeth. The taste was both astringent and slightly sweet. Robyn followed suit, though she kept her eyes on Gerallt, waiting for the next instruction. Alma tried to chew on one side of her mouth, eager to avoid incurring the blotchy green smile Gerallt had flashed.

After a few minutes of this, Gerallt leaned over the pot on the stove and spat the contents of his mouth into it. By that time, Alma was only too eager to do likewise. The wet globules sizzled on the hot pebbles. Her mouth felt inexplicably dry, considering she'd been chewing for so long. She used her finger to scrape as much remnant green out as she could, and flicked it into the pot, pulling a face.

"What was that?" she asked.

"Something for focus," Gerallt said. "It heightens the senses you need and dulls the ones you don't."

Alma scanned the room, using the contrast between the light of the candles and the dark corners to assess if she was experiencing anything. Aside from feeling slightly parched in her mouth, everything seemed normal as she moved her head.

"You getting anything from that?" she asked Robyn while Gerallt used a palette knife to spread the paste they'd created together.

Robyn looked up and waggled her head thoughtfully. "Not sure. A little buzzed, maybe. Mostly, I feel like I need to brush my teeth."

Alma nodded and gave a slightly uncontrolled laugh, accompanied by a mild sense of elation. Perhaps the nasty green stuff was doing something after all.

Gerallt ignored them and formed his hands into a bowl. He remained still for a moment with his eyes closed. "The Evil Eye is upon one of you. To listen clearly, we must remove its oppression."

Alma immediately thought back to the picture of the goat in Damien's office, with its sinister, staring eyes. Could that have been the 'evil eye' Gerallt was referring to? She derailed her own train of thought by picturing how she must have looked to Damien when he walked in on her having a staring contest with the framed print. Immediately she snorted, trying a little harder this time to stifle her amusement. She could hear Robyn fighting a fit of giggles also.

Gerallt opened another of the boxes. It released a distinctive smell as he pinched something out of it, then sprinkled some black grains onto a cigarette paper he took from his pocket. Alma thought they looked like onion seeds. He folded the paper into a parcel, which he twisted closed, then shifted onto his knees and shuffled around until he was positioned behind Robyn.

69

"Protect from the Eye which has looked on you for harm," Gerallt said, reaching around and holding the little paper parcel in front of Robyn's face. He passed it over her, down to her knees, and brought it up again. "Protect with light that is pure and loving. She rejects the Evil Eye, send it away from her."

Robyn remained still until Gerallt finished. A silence lingered, and she looked at Alma with tight lips, unsure what to do and still trying not to laugh. "Amen?"

"So mote it be," Alma said, smiling.

Robyn took a breath to compose herself, closed her eyes, and repeated the words. "So mote it be."

Gerallt then repositioned himself to kneel behind Alma and repeated the ritual. Alma kept her eyes closed, trying to focus on the words and not on the sculpted arms loosely encircling her.

"So mote it be." Alma spoke the antiphon and opened her eyes. Gerallt's hand settled on her shoulder. His long fingers tingled, like rain dripping down her back.

"There," he said. "The oppression is lifted."

Alma's lips parted as Gerallt returned to his place across the stove from them. The question she wanted to ask had been lingering since he'd mentioned the Evil Eye. Yet when she tried to give it voice, she was too afraid.

Was it really gone?

She glanced at Robyn, who was no longer swallowing giggles.

Gerallt sat and cupped his hands over the stove again, dropping the little parcel of seeds into it. "Now we will ask the gods and spirits to give us guidance. I cannot

70

guarantee who will respond to our invitation, but we may receive better if we lay out what it is we seek."

Robyn laid a hand on Alma's arm. "You should ask about your brother. Ask if he really knows where you..."

Alma put a finger to her lip. "*Shh.* Let's not give him *too* much to work with. But yes, alright. Ask what I should do about my brother."

Gerallt hummed and closed his eyes for half a minute or so. "Something is here. It's telling me that you are afraid."

"Afraid of my brother?" Alma asked, trying to keep her voice flat and devoid of clues. But Gerallt's eyes were still closed; he wasn't trying to read her.

After another pause, Gerallt's mouth curved up at the corner. "No. Not your brother. Our visitor is showing me someone else."

Alma looked into the pot. Her chest felt suddenly tight and the dryness in her mouth was becoming unbearable. An image of Ryan formed in her head. She held her breath and clenched her jaw shut to keep hold of the thought and resist the temptation to speak his name.

"A woman," Gerallt continued. "Young, short blonde hair. Someone you don't know by name."

Alma gulped, but her throat was so parched that she gagged instead. Her heart was hammering. "What about her?"

"She saw your deepest fear this morning. On the train. And now you are afraid that it has given her power over you."

The room, which had been so decidedly cool when they'd entered, now felt stifling. Alma tugged at her sweater, trying to release some of the heat. Robyn was staring, her mouth hanging open.

"Who is telling you this?" Alma asked.

Gerallt opened his eyes to look at her, but said nothing. He opened yet another box and reached in with both hands, taking out a gnarled, capped grey stem in each. Mushrooms.

"Our friend wishes to know: are you here to be convinced, or to experience and receive?"

Alma frowned and took the mushroom. Gerallt gave the other to Robyn and took a third for himself.

"This is how you get the spirits to speak?" Alma asked.

"Nature gives us the means to make our minds a blank canvas," Gerallt said. "In silence, imagination and confusion paint on our canvas. But in the presence of a spirit…"

Robyn shifted edgily in her place. "Are you kidding? That's not hearing spirits, that's just tripping."

Gerallt shot her a look and gestured towards Alma. "Today, a blonde girl deliberately frightened her after witnessing her in a state of deepest terror on the train. This girl, willingly or not, is now a focus for this deepest fear she carries. A spirit is waiting to show you how to be freed of this, but first, we must have the vision."

Alma looked at the mushroom in her hand, and saw that it was trembling. Around the thrumming of her own heartbeat in her ears, she thought she could discern whispers, yet no amount of straining could make them clearer.

She pushed it into her mouth and chewed until able to swallow. Gerallt took at the same time, then Robyn after a brief hesitation. Alma took slow, deliberate breaths and looked at the ground, watching for it to take effect.

Several minutes of silence passed. Instead of becoming more intelligible, the whispers seemed to fade. The heartbeat in her ears receded. Alma felt calm. In the corner of her eye, she noticed Robyn shedding her cardigan. Underneath was a white vest and lots of flushed pink skin. Was it really that warm in here?

"This spirit is powerful," Gerallt said. His words came out like they should have been framed in a big red triangle. "It is able to carry a curse away and place it on the shoulders of another. This girl you met, in exploiting your fear, has made herself a candidate for this curse."

"I thought witchcraft was supposed to be about goodwill and blessings," Robyn said. "Why does anybody need to be cursed?"

Gerallt didn't answer her. He was staring at Alma. "What would you have the spirit do?"

Alma didn't know what to say. Her shoulders felt like they were lifting, and forced her breathing to steady, grounding herself. The orange and brown pattern of the carpet became fluid, the colours swirling. She reached down, but couldn't bring herself to touch it, lest she fall in.

She squeezed her eyes tightly, then opened them. All around her, little brown stems grew out of the carpet. She gasped and wrapped her arms around herself. She wanted to tell herself this wasn't real. But if it wasn't real, then that meant the hope sprouting in her heart also wasn't real. A hope that maybe she would finally be free. A hope that she wouldn't have to be afraid anymore.

73

It was impossible to say how long she stared at the carpet considering this. Perhaps a minute, perhaps ten. Eventually, Gerallt repeated the question, his voice a manifestation of gentle patience.

"What would you have the spirit do?"

Alma lifted her eyes to meet his, which seemed to have a faint green glow. The face of his 'Green Man' tattoo, previously frowning, was now smiling. A sense of weightlessness took her.

"I will take back my curse," she said. "And I pass on a blessing. I forgive the girl who did me ill, and wish for her peace and happiness. For her, and also for my brother." A chuckle escaped, and she added, "And also for the lovely dog I met at work today."

Gerallt's smile grew until it was as broad as that of the beaming face on his chest. He held his arms out to the side and angled his head back.

"So mote it be," he said. "Light banishes the dark. Life conquers death. Love defeats hate. The spirit has heard your wish. Now may it go and deliver."

Alma laughed nervously and glanced across at Robyn.

"Was that the right answer?" Robyn asked.

"There is no right answer," Gerallt said. "There is only the truth in your heart. The spirit has heard your truth and will act accordingly."

Alma exhaled and held her hands open just above the shimmering surface of the liquid carpet. "Love is the real truth. That is what we believed in my old circle."

Robyn shifted and straightened her legs out in front of her. As she set her feet down, patches of orange grass burst from the carpet around them. Alma laughed and brushed the carpet to see if the same thing would happen

74

at her touch. Instead, brown, vine-like tendrils snaked up in the wake of her hand.

"So what happens now?" Robyn asked, leaning back on her elbows and looking peaceful.

"We thank the spirit," Gerallt sighed, his eyes still glowing. "We show our gratitude and sincerity by becoming the embodiment of love."

Something swirled in Alma's chest, and a guffaw jumped out of her mouth.

"Sounds like that works out pretty well for you," she said. Her attempted haughtiness was betrayed by her gaze running over his long, lean arms spread wide.

Gerallt closed his arms until they were both stretched out towards Alma. Then he slowly moved them to point at Robyn. "You two."

Alma's mouth parted in surprise. She expected another laugh to come tumbling out, but as she looked over at Robyn, she saw that a flowering bed of orange grass and moss spread all around her, the brown sprigs growing upwards and undulating like beckoning fingers.

Robyn gave Alma a quizzical look and sat upright. "Are you alright?"

Alma crawled towards her, being careful to find the firm patches on the liquid floor. The wriggling brown vines tickled her arms and legs. She reached Robyn, whose chest and shoulders were even more red and flustered now. Alma pursed her lips…and blew on Robyn like she was a cup of hot tea, then immediately dissolved into giggles.

"What's happening?" Robyn asked, grinning widely and sitting upright. "That feels nice. Lovely and cool."

Alma took a deep breath to swallow her laughter, looking Robyn in the eye for focus. She shuffled closer still and pursed her lips again, this time leaning all the way in to press them against Robyn's.

Robyn pushed herself up on both arms into the kiss. Something slipped around Alma's shoulder. She realised it was the brown vines. She could feel them pushing her and Robyn together, slipping underneath her sweater, exposing a sliver of skin to the refreshingly cool air and reminding her how uncomfortably warm she was.

Alma lifted her arms and allowed the sweater to be pulled off. When it was gone, she saw Robyn was up on her knees now, a glazed smile on her face.

"So nice and cool..." Robyn whispered, leaning in for another kiss. As she did, the light from the candles seemed to mottle and fade, as though behind textured glass. Around her, the brown vines were growing into trees, blossoming with their approval.

From behind her, two more branches snaked around her waist and pulled her back against a solid trunk, like a pair of long, lean arms holding her against a solid, smiling chest.

Chapter 8

Heavy clouds rolled across pale greys, pinks and blues of the Anglesea sunset. Rain was on the way.

Perhaps it would wash the bloodstains from the window cill.

Perhaps the arguing would stop before the clouds arrived, and all of this would go away.

Alma held her arms over her chest, her tiny fingers interlocking over the wooden crucifix she'd been given from the wall. A hedgehog hand-puppet she'd found in the playroom was flattened against her, stopping the wooden corners of the cross digging in. Lying in bed, her eyes never left the window. Nothing was there now. If she could convince herself — or lie to everyone else — that there had been nothing there at all, she could put an end to all the trouble.

But she *had* seen it, was still seeing it. What frightened her more was the feeling that it could still see her.

The shouting was just outside the bedroom door. Her father always sounded angry when he was speaking in Lithuanian. Alma didn't know what he was saying: that was the only reason her family ever spoke Lithuanian. But she'd learned to tell when the anger was real.

Today, it was real.

While her gaze guarded the window, her ears trawled for words she recognised.

"Dėl Dievo meilės! Vesk ją čia. Ji mus gėdina."

Ji. 'She'. Father was talking about her. Probably about her staying in bed and refusing to come to dinner. She'd made the decision long before that horrible thing had appeared in the window. They were serving goat. *The*

77

goat. But her father wasn't concerned about what happened; he just wanted to avoid embarrassment.

Her mother came next. She spoke quickly, pragmatically and with less emotion. "Filip, mes tau atleisime jei pasakysi tiesą! Ar tu padėjai tą baisų dalyką ant palangės?"

Alma recognised her brother's name and a question beginning "did you". Mother was trying to get him to tell her what had happened. Possibly to ascertain the truth; more likely to assuage Father's frustration.

Filip's response was sullen and slurred. Alma didn't understand a word, but she could hear resentment in every syllable. The only thing she could be sure of was that he wasn't admitting to putting the goat's head on the window cill. He wouldn't admit to it even if he was guilty, but Alma wondered if he was even that stupid. Filip had already been screamed at for sending her into that dirty grey room with the dead goat, hanging there with blood still dripping from its slit neck.

"Tai ar nori pasakyti, kad tai Ryan padarė?" It was her mother again, asking if it had been Ryan that did it. Filip evidently wasn't admitting to anything. Alma didn't want to believe that possibility. Ryan said he was her friend. Filip had never been her friend. He was her brother. He always told her it was his job to look out for her, but not to *like* her.

"Iš kur aš žinau?" Filip was spitting his words now. "Ta durna maža kalė tikriausiai tai išsigalvojo, kad mus į bėdą pasodintų."

Alma shrank into the pillow propped up behind her and lifted the hedgehog puppet's face to her chin. *Maža kalė* — she knew those words. It was Lithuanian for 'Alma'.

Her brother used it all the time. They were the only Lithuanian words he ever spoke to her directly. He'd never said it in front of their parents until now.

"Nesikeik prie savo mamos." Father's words were accompanied by a sharp slap and a hiss of pain from Filip. "Nebent nori gaut lupt! Dabar greit prie stalo."

Lupt. 'Thrashing'. Father was threatening Filip with a beating. Almost certainly for using foul language rather than for the goat's head prank. The prospect of a thrashing always sounded terrifying from Father: enough to pacify them almost every time. She'd only known him to make good on the threat a couple of times — always on Filip, never on her. The idea of beating was all the more frightening because she'd never experienced one.

Ryan got beatings from his father, too. They didn't sound half as scary. Ryan almost seemed proud of them. He said it made him respect his father. Alma wasn't sure what Ryan got beaten for, though. With Filip, it was obvious. Perhaps if Filip was beaten more often, he'd be more like Ryan.

Hurried footsteps moved away down the hall outside, while Mother and Father continued muttering to each other. The room darkened as the clouds arrived. Alma couldn't make out any words now. They faded underneath the pattering on the window.

The rain quickly became heavy against the glass. If she used her imagination, she could see all sorts of things in the window now. Ghosts, faces, hands. She knew they weren't real — that she was making them up. She tried to conjure an image of the staring eyes of the dead goat in the window, and found she couldn't. It couldn't be imagined. Only remembered.

Mother had assured her it was just a prank. Father had tried to suggest she'd fallen asleep and dreamt it. Eventually, her parents moved away from the door and she was alone. The feeling that it was still looking at her remained. Was she imagining that? Perhaps.

But if the haunting eyes had just been a prank or a dream, why had her mother taken the crucifix from the wall for Alma to hold, and told her it would protect her?

Alma stared at the window until long after everyone else had gone to bed. She didn't want to take her eyes away whilst something was watching, though she saw nothing but the watery shapes sliding down the glass pane, like bodies falling under gunfire.

When she eventually fell asleep, she saw for the first time the watching, inhuman eyes. Staring. Following. Blood running from underneath a pointed chin.

And before the sun came up, she woke with a scream, clasping her throat.

It came as more of a ragged gasp this time. Alma arched and flattened her hands either side of her, finding no purchase on the threadbare carpet that itched her legs and shoulders. The cold air rushed on her as though it had been waiting for her to wake. Her mouth and throat felt desiccated.

Usually, when it happened, she'd pull a cushion or a bunch of her covers against her chest and stare at a window until she was sure the eyes weren't looking. But there were no covers. The window was boarded over. There was some morning light leaking through from the hallway.

Alma pushed herself up with one aching, shivering arm. Her other hand gripped her amulets, and she realised the necklace was the only thing she was wearing.

It was freezing. Robyn lay nearby, on her side, with one arm under her head and the other outstretched, like she'd fallen asleep with the arm draped over something. Their clothes were scattered about. The candles had long burnt out. The gas stove and the pot remained, but offered no warmth.

It was only the two of them in the room. The house was silent.

She dressed as quickly and quietly as she could. Her clothes felt frigid on her body at first. They rubbed uncomfortably against her skin, irritated by the scratchy carpet. As she pulled her trousers on, she went into the pocket for her phone to check the time. It wasn't there. Had she left it at the flat? Maybe. There had been no number to call on the flyer, so the last time she'd seen it was when she'd shown it to Robyn on the sofa yesterday.

She zipped her jacket up to the neck and willed her body to warm the inside of it. She collected Robyn's clothes and draped them over her. A gentle patting of her shoulder was enough to rouse her. Robyn's groan was reedy and dry. Alma moved away and faced the door.

"What time is it?" Robyn croaked.

"I'm not sure. I don't have my phone. It's morning."

Robyn creaked up into a sitting position and the clothes fell away. "Oh, hello. Yup, I'm naked. That happened."

Hastily, she fumbled the vest over her head. Alma cautiously peered out of the room. She could see a kitchen at the end of the hall. Apart from the sound of Robyn dressing, all was silent. Venturing out, she found the kitchen utterly barren, except for an overflowing ashtray on the worktop. There was no water from the tap, and no glasses — or anything else — in the cupboards. Alma's throat felt like candle wax every time she swallowed.

"No water or electricity," she called to Robyn, returning to the lounge, with no interest in exploring upstairs and a growing compulsion to leave. "Are you alright? Can you stand?"

Robyn remained sat on the floor, tying the laces of her Doc Martens. "Yeah, fine. That was not what I expected. Is that the kind of thing you used to get up to?"

"Not at all. I'd have warned you if I'd known it was going to get *that* weird."

"Where is Mr Mystical? Is it too much to hope he's out there making us breakfast like a gentleman?"

"I don't know. Maybe upstairs. Maybe gone. I'm not waiting around to find out."

Robyn climbed to her feet and patted herself down. Alma approached the front door. It was dim outside; the streetlights were still on. She couldn't hear any cars or people yet. When Robyn joined her, they both stepped outside and pulled the door softly behind them. It was scarcely cooler outside than in. Alma looked down the well-presented terrace that politely ignored the scruffy tramp of a house at the end of the row.

"There's a shop just this way," Robyn said, pointing up the road. "I'm dying for a drink. Then a long, hot shower."

She stepped away, but Alma stayed put. She could just about make out the sounds of traffic over the trees at the bottom of the terrace. A worn wood-path led in that direction, and she deduced it would take her towards Penglais hill.

"I don't think I've got time to go home," she said. "The university is that way, right?"

"You're actually going to work?" Robyn screwed up her face. "Don't. Throw a sicky."

"I think I should go. Damien excused me for most of my first day so I could set myself up. I can't cry off sick on my second day."

"Right, I suppose you need to maintain a professional image." Robyn looked Alma up and down as she said that. Alma tried not to imagine how she must look.

"As best as I can under the circumstances."

"Fair enough." Robyn paused uncertainly. "Can we agree Damien doesn't need to know about us getting off our tits on mushrooms and having a three-way in a squat house?"

"Um, yes, I think that would be best." Alma's face burned as she tried not to let images of last night flash into her mind. Mercifully, much of it was obscured in any case.

Robyn dug out her phone and shook her head. Out of battery, unsurprisingly. She looked up at Alma as the both of them wondered what they were lingering for.

"I, uh, hope this doesn't make it awkward," Robyn said. "I'm still happy for you to move in. When I said we should go out and get to know each other as flatmates, I didn't quite mean it to go like that."

"It's alright." Alma breathed out and smiled. Robyn visibly relaxed. "We are disciples of experience. Let's chalk it up to that."

"Sounds good to me. I'll see you this evening, then?"

"Sure. Maybe just pasta and a movie this time."

"Perfect."

Leaving Robyn to walk past the houses full of people with their normal lives, Alma turned towards the path and rubbed her face. She had no mirror to check for red eyes or smeared mascara, or any marks or bruises for that matter. Nothing on her face *felt* sore. Heavy smoke lingered on her sweater.

The path twisted through the trees, and she could hear the main road some way ahead. A little way in, there was a depression in the trees where some pallets and planks were set up as bike ramps. Further in, a log hung from a branch by a rope. Alma smiled, allocating all her thoughts to remembering the days of playing in the scrubland near the estate where she grew up. Or exploring the fields around Ryan's parents' farm. Or going into the woods with her coven as a teenager on Shabbat festival evenings to build a campfire and cast spells.

She considered the log as it got closer. Perhaps it was a swing, but why wouldn't they have hung it in the clearing, where there was more space? It also seemed too large for kids to have put up by themselves.

Pondering this helped keep her mind off other things she didn't want to think about. In the broken light, it was just a dark shape, but it gave her something to mark up ahead.

The first suspicion came when she noticed something bushy hanging from the top end of the object, dirty and yellow. She cursed and walked quicker, eager to prove her imagination wrong. But gradually her stomach began to twist with horrible realisation. Her arms felt cold and weak, but her legs carried her forwards as though just another step might make it all seem different.

It was the naked body of a woman hanging from a rope tied under her shoulders. A long trail of mostly dried blood ran down her entire body from her throat. A short curtain of tangled blond hair partially obscured her face. Even so, Alma could see enough to recognise the face she'd seen several times yesterday, and once in the horrific visions that had pulled her from sleep that morning.

Chapter 9

Alma worked her cluster of pendants in her hand while the police detective scribbled on his pad. The fear was paralysing. The worst part was not being sure she wasn't responsible for this.

With her head half-bowed, she looked towards the path through the woods, now sealed off with police tape. Her fingertips crept up to her collar, touching the pit above her sternum. The inside of her throat felt sandblasted.

"Thank you, Miss Petrulytė," the detective said. His musical Welsh accent sounded inappropriately jovial. "Where had you been before you discovered the body?"

Alma glanced over her shoulder at the derelict house.

"I was at home," she said.

"And where is that?"

Alma failed to remember the name of the road, so rummaged in her jacket pocket for the scrap of paper. "Number Two Rheidol Terrace."

The detective seemed confused by her hesitation, and did not immediately write it down. "That's where you live?"

"Yes. But I only moved in yesterday. That's why…" She showed him the piece of paper.

"And where were you going?"

"To work. Penglais Campus."

The detective hummed and scribbled. "Rheidol Terrace, that's by the harbour, isn't it? This isn't on the way to the campus from the harbour."

Alma grasped her necklace, cursing herself. "I was a little lost. As I say, I only moved to the area a couple of days ago. I slept badly last night, left for work early and ended up taking the long route."

Her voice cracked as she spoke. These questions were difficult. Even more than the ones which had required her to describe the corpse and the injuries. Alma struggled to maintain eye contact with the detective and looked towards the path again. She imagined that if she stared through the trees long enough, she'd still be able to see the body hanging there.

Behind her, people were emerging from their homes. She felt their muttering all over her back and hoped one of the other police officers would send them back inside. An excitable child's voice asked his mother what was happening. Alma shut her eyes tight. *How easily a child could have been first up that path...*

Just as she felt her strength about to collapse, resigning her to admit everything about the previous night, the detective put his notepad away and took out a small card from his pocket with a number and the name 'Det Insp Clifford'.

"Thanks for being patient, Miss Petrulytė," he said. "If you think of anything else, you can call this number. I can have someone give you a lift somewhere if you like."

"No, thanks...I..." Alma watched as two officers ducked under the police tape. "Is that it? What happens now?"

"Well, our priority will be to identify the young woman and find out who else was in the area. You said you hadn't seen the victim before?"

Alma's gaze slipped back towards the woods. The terrified, ashen face, peering through dried-straw hair, appeared in her mind. She shook her head, knowing full well that too was a lie.

Damien didn't seem to notice Alma's barely-tamed hair, dark eyes or the fact that she was wearing the same clothes as yesterday. He was far too excited by the news about the body found in the woods next to the Dan-y-Coed estate, and whether she'd heard about it.

It didn't seem strange that he knew. Alma found it more odd that Damien didn't know she was the one who found the body. That he couldn't smell it on her. The dead girl's presence hung about her like a stench.

Alma could do nothing but sit and listen, glad at least that she wasn't being asked how she got on with the reading material, or with meeting Robyn. All of that was old news to Damien, who was so animated in his speculating and sensationalising that Flick frequently hopped up as if she thought he was about to throw a ball.

Alma took out the growing collection of cards and paper from her pocket. DI Clifford's contact card was at the front. Everything she had chosen not to disclose hung around her neck like a millstone. But did it matter? If she called the police now, what more could she tell them? That she had invoked a spirit to impart blessing on a stranger she'd met on the train? And now that stranger was dead. What would the police do with that information?

Alma shuffled the card to the back. The next in the sequence were her train tickets. She'd prayed a blessing for her brother too, just like she'd promised on the phone. Had that prayer had consequences also? For the first time in as long as she remembered, she felt the urge to call Filip. She still didn't want to see him, or for him to know where she was, but she at least wanted to know he was alive.

The next was Ryan's card. Without the contacts saved on her phone, he was the only person whose number she had, apart from the detective's.

"Hey, are you alright?" Damien said, suddenly discontent with having the conversation by himself. It was as though he could sense who she was thinking about and had moved to intervene. "You seem a little off."

Alma bit her lip, annoyed that he presumed to know her well enough to say if she was 'off'.

"Sorry. I didn't want to say anything because I'm not sure if I'm supposed to. I'm the one who discovered that body this morning."

Damien's face dropped and froze with undisguised fascination in his eyes. "Holy shit, I'm so sorry. There's me going on about it."

His mouth flapped as the questions he really wanted to ask tried to lurch out. "When did…" "Was it…" He swallowed each of them down just in time and settled on the more sympathetic question of why she was even at work after something like that. Alma explained she didn't want to not turn up on her second day.

Damien insisted on getting her out of the office and buying her a coffee, which was a welcome gesture under the circumstances. Flick jumped up, tail wagging.

Damien told her to stay and left her standing expectantly as he closed the office door behind them.

There was a cafeteria in the Arts Centre, but Damien thought it would be better to go a little further up the hill to Brynamlwg: a pub operated by the university. At that time in the morning, there would be fewer students around. Alma filled a glass of water from a glass water dispenser, then took a small corner table while Damien got the coffees.

"So, do the police need you to do anything else today?" he asked before his backside even touched the seat.

"I don't know. They just said they're going to begin enquiries."

She avoided meeting his eye, but the pub offered little distraction. There was a long canvas depicting the Last Supper rendered in a surreal cartoon style, which reminded her of the Beatles film, *The Yellow Submarine*. She couldn't find anything about it that would be worthy of starting a conversation. It was a shame the dog wasn't with them as an excusable diversion.

"I can't imagine what it must have been like, just finding something like that," Damien said, shaking his head and pretending he wasn't probing her to *tell* him what it was like.

"It was horrible. I'm trying not to think about it."

"Mm, of course. I'm sure. It must be harder being new here and not having anyone to lean on. But I want you to know that you can always…"

Alma cut him off. "Actually, Robyn and I hit it off really well. Thanks so much for the tip. She's great. I feel like I have a friend already."

Damien had that crestfallen peacock look about him again. "Perfect. Great news. I knew you would."

Alma wondered if Robyn had heard the news yet. More likely, she was asleep. She tried desperately to rationalise the coincidences. How could Gerallt have known those things about her brother, or the girl on the train?

She thought of all the times she'd met with her friends to invoke the spirits, gods and goddesses, and had come away convinced that they'd received a sign or a message. Had any of those occasions been as direct and compelling as last night?

"I'm sorry," she said. "I'm probably not very good company. I hope you don't think I'm being rude."

"It's fine, honestly. You've had a hell of an ordeal. If there's anything I can do to help, just say."

Alma smiled and finished her drink. "The coffee is a help. Thank you. I think the best thing is to carry on as normal. Not give myself too much space to think."

"Absolutely. Well, if it keeps your mind off things, why don't we go back to the office and I'll get your thoughts on a lecture I'm giving this afternoon? Then, if you like, you could sit in on the lecture and get a feel for the class."

It sounded like a good plan, so Alma let him lead the way back to campus. A light drizzle had started outside. The moisture in the air was an antidote to the dryness in her throat, which remained even after a coffee and several glasses of water. She turned her face up and breathed it in, wishing it could become a shower to wash the previous night away.

The walk took them past the residence halls. A police car was parked up on the bank. Groups of students sat on

92

the steps outside, some with their heads in their hands. One tearful girl was on her phone.

Alma suddenly lowered her face, hoping that her curtain of ash-silver hair would make her disappear into the grey of the cloudy day. She couldn't have been more on edge if she'd cut the young woman's throat herself.

She kept her head down all the way to Damien's office door. Alma braced herself in anticipation of Flick's scrabbling paws, but the door opened quietly.

"So the lecture this afternoon is called 'Should immoral art works repel us?'" Damien went straight to the computer. "It's a bit philosophy-heavy, but I think you'll find it interesting."

Alma persuaded herself that was possible, remembering how engaging Damien had sounded when they had only communicated by email. She paced the length of the room while he looked for the file. Her eyes were on the alcove in the far corner, where the Sabbatic Goat was lurking out of sight. She wanted to look it in the eye, and know that it was just picture: not an evil spirit who had spoken to her through Gerallt and then murdered an innocent woman.

She rounded the corner, ready to confront it — then cried out in horror. Reeling out of the narrow space, her foot caught on the leg of a desk and she toppled, crashing painfully against a chair as she went down. The rebuke she had prepared to whisper swelled in her throat, choking her.

"Woah, are you alright?" Damien jumped up and hurried over. He quickly offered his hand, but when he turned to look into the alcove, his arm dropped limp and he let out a pathetic whimper.

93

The goat print was on the floor, propped against the wall. Blood now ran down the middle of the figure's chest, between its breasts, appearing as though it was trickling from the creature's throat. The actual source of the blood was Flick's headless body, which was suspended, pierced on the hook from which the picture had hung.

"This can't be real." The words came from Alma as a breath. She shifted onto her knees, reading the words which had been crudely written in blood in the spaces on either side of the Sabbatic Goat.

Do you get what you pray for?

Clutching her ribs where she'd impacted against the chair, she pulled herself up. Damien was clutching his head, staring at the desecrated remains of his dog. Alma wanted to flee from the room, but the grief and agony on his face stayed her fear. She hobbled a step closer and touched his arm.

"Damien, my god I'm so…"

She wasn't prepared for him to slap her arm away and bear towards her, red faced and manic. "What the hell is this?" he yelled. "Is this you?"

Alma gaped, momentarily nonplussed. "I…how could I have done it? I was with you!"

"All your talk about goats and hell and witchcraft, is this some sort of pantomime to you? Are you trying to scare people into thinking it's all real?"

"Damien, what are you talking about? Are you being serious? Of course I had nothing to do with this! I would never…"

Damien growled and span away, violently kicking a filing cabinet which clanged and rattled like a snare drum. He clutched at his hair, turning this way and that as though looking for a direction to evacuate his rage.

"Why the fuck would someone do this to my dog? Just get out! If I find out that you and your fucking witchy devil worship friends had anything to do with this…" His faculty of reason seemed to kick in mid-tirade. His teeth were bared, and he was rocking back and forth under the momentum of sheer emotion. "…just…just leave. I'll sort this out. You just need to go."

Alma slid along the desk, moving away from Damien's furious panting and the grisly diorama in the alcove. She looked at the writing one more time. Another drop of blood fell from the body and splattered onto the middle of the Sabbatic Goat's chest.

Quickly, she pushed away and made for the door. There was nowhere left on the campus where the sense of guilt couldn't find her. Even when she was alone in the corridor, she felt eyes watching, as though from a distance. She shut her eyes tight, closing her fingers around her pendants. *I am here, I am now, and I can make peace with this moment.* But the words sounded utterly ridiculous in her own ears. There was no peace to be found.

Hurrying through the Arts Centre, she emerged onto the forecourt of the Student Union, where students herded in several directions. Several of them glanced warily at Alma, and she realised she had one hand over her mouth and the other arm tightly wrapped around herself. It was still drizzling.

Down the steps and onto the road, she was at least out of sight from the crowd of students. She made it as far as the reception building, where the campus service road

95

joined the main road down Penglais Hill towards the town. Her lungs were caving in, and she could go no further; not with the eyes on her back, narrowed in mockery.

As she stumbled into the reception lobby, she almost collided head on with a police officer. She froze and looked him in the eye. He wasn't anyone she recognised from the crime scene, nor did he seem to recognise her. He stepped aside and held an arm out for her to pass. "Whoops. Careful there."

Alma thinned her lips to squeeze any treacherous expression from her face and nodded. She shuffled past the officer and up to the desk. The man sitting behind it was grim-faced and solemn, like someone who might have been assisting the police with an investigation into the murder of a campus resident. There was no smile present, even as he looked up to ask if he could help.

"Could I possibly use a phone, please?" Alma asked, her voice as flat as the man's expression.

When a telephone was placed up on the counter, she pulled out the contents of her coat pocket again, picked up the receiver, and dialled the only number she had that didn't belong to a police officer.

Chapter 10

Alma had never seen the inside of The Academy during daylight hours. She remembered evenings when the hall was filled with club music and students drinking three-pound vodka Red Bulls. But right now, the dominant sound was the driving rain against the arch windows. She ran her fingers through her hair, trying to comb out what little of the downpour she'd been unlucky to be caught in.

From a table on the mezzanine floor, she looked down at the bar where Ryan was ordering their drinks. Had there always been a full set of church organ pipes behind the spirits shelves? In the old days, it must always have been too crowded — or she herself been too intoxicated — for her to notice the club was converted from an old chapel. There was even a pulpit built into the bannister of the stairs up to the mezzanine.

"It's not often the devil gives way to God," Ryan said when she asked him if he knew anything about it. That, he explained, was apparently what the Aberystwyth Observer had remarked in 1855 when a pub on the site had been shut down for keeping 'improper hours', and a Methodist church had taken its place.

"And now it's a student bar," Alma said, taking a swig from her bottle. "I guess the devil took his seat back after all."

"Simple economics really. There are more students in Aberystwyth than churchgoers."

Alma wondered why he said it in such a matter-of-fact way, as though the impiety of the town troubled him less than it ought to. It was a shame he couldn't have been so indifferent about her own apostasy when they were younger.

Yet his understated, affable smile soothed her anxiety. Finally, her lungs were not strung tightly and her hands were not shaking.

"Which church do you serve at?" It wasn't something she cared to know. She wanted to pretend there was no white collar on his neck. "The big one over the way? St Mary's? Or that cool little one on the hill?"

"That little chapel does belong to the diocese as it happens. I have a key to it."

"Really? What's it like in there?"

"Cold. But peaceful. I go there occasionally for a little quiet time."

"To pray?"

"I've no shortage of places to pray. No, I go there to think."

A scoff tumbled from Alma's lips. "I'd never thought of church as a place to 'think'."

Ryan smiled. "God interrupts you less often than people do."

"That makes sense."

Ryan hadn't asked why Alma chose to call him, or what had happened. Now he looked at her patiently, inviting her to tell him when she was ready.

She wasn't ready. Not yet.

"It's complicated actually," he said, eventually. "Our church in town — St Winefride's on Queens Road — was shut down because of structural concerns. So now we have a smaller church. Welsh Martyrs out in Penparcau. The parishioners hate it; it's all a bit political."

98

"I guess that's the kind of ball-ache you sign up for when you become a priest."

"Amen," Ryan said wistfully, throwing back his beer.

Once again, he left a space for her to say whatever was on her mind. But Alma wasn't sure what that was. Where should she begin? Did she want to tell him about the events of that morning? Of the previous night? Of the past eight years?

"Did you hear about the student who was murdered?" she asked.

"I did. Very sad. Aber's always been such a safe place. You just don't expect something like that here."

"I was the one who found her body in the woods. I was walking to work at the time."

Ryan looked at her with a calm and kindness that must come from working in certain professions. "I'm really sorry. That must have been awful. How are you feeling about it?"

"Guilty."

"What on earth should you feel guilty about?"

Alma tested the words in her head first. They sounded crazy enough before she said them out loud, yet she committed to them anyway. "The girl who was killed is the girl we saw coming out of the cafe yesterday. The one I had the run in on the train with. I prayed for her last night. For forgiveness and blessing. And then this morning she turns up dead."

Ryan tugged at the white slip in his collar. Alma wished he would just pull it out and be Ryan again. Then she would be comfortable.

"That's an unfortunate coincidence. You don't believe that your prayer and her death are linked, though, do you?"

The reversal of the situation was intolerable: a *priest* was trying to convince *her* that a circumstance did not have a supernatural cause. That was not how she'd imagined this going.

"You were the first person to tell me paganism was a way of inviting the devil into your life. Are you saying you don't believe in curses anymore?"

Ryan shrugged. "In principle, yes. But, like the Church, I believe these things must be weighed and tested. Too often, religion is muddied by popular superstition."

"I've never been religious *or* superstitious, Ryan. And it wasn't paganism or witchcraft that haunted me all my life. It was…"

Her words ground to a halt. Ryan set his drink on the table and knit his hands together, leaning closer.

"You're talking about the goat, aren't you?"

"I don't know," Alma said. But what she meant was that she didn't know what else it could be. Night after night of horrible visions, year after year. The tragedy that struck like lightning time after time whenever she dropped her guard.

And now this.

"It stopped for years. And now it's back. Someone I named in a ritual is dead. Is that superstition?"

Her hand hovered by her neck again. Ryan watched her turning her pendants over in her fingers and checking her throat for wounds.

"You told me you believed witchcraft gave you the power to resist the curse," he said.

"It made me feel safe after Filip left. It kept the visions away. Bad things stopped happening around me. I don't have beliefs and I don't have a religion, but I acknowledge results."

"No religion, you say?" Ryan's mouth curled a little. Alma felt her stomach knot. "You've got quite a little collection of symbols around your neck for someone with no religion."

"Symbols aren't gods."

"Indeed. Is that the Cross of St Benedict I see there?"

Without looking, Alma found the heavy round cross he was referring to, pinched it out of the cluster and held it up.

"Patron saint of protection against evil," she said.

"I know. And how do you think the father of western monasticism would feel about being bunched up in between Hecate's Wheel and the Seal of Mohammed?"

"I think he'd say you can never have too many friends," Alma retorted. "Listen to you. How did you go from being a happy clappy evangelical who believed Catholics aren't real Christians, to sticking up for a Catholic Saint pendant?"

Ryan shrugged. "I was wrong, and I'm happy to admit it. I've always followed the truth where it leads, not where it's convenient."

Alma dropped the pendant and folded her arms on the table. "Or maybe you're just following *me*. You gave me grief for having a Catholic upbringing; now I've moved on from that and you're a Catholic priest. Maybe your next stop will be pragmatic agnosticism."

"What a fascinating term. What do you think it means?"

"It means that I don't know what's really out there and neither do you."

Ryan nodded slowly. "And that's what you are so scared about. Because you don't know what's out there."

Alma wasn't sure what made her turn towards the window and look down at the road. The rain came down heavily. Every dark recess and corner seemed to move. She looked back at Ryan, hating that, of the two of them, he sounded the most rational.

"I want to believe there's nothing," she said. "All I've ever wanted was for any gods or angels or spirits out there to stay away."

"So you wear them all around your neck?"

"You say St Benedict would be jealous of the others? Maybe they all would be. Maybe that's why I keep them together: to try to offend them all enough to leave me alone."

Ryan tilted his head. "I think I might be starting to get a sense of how that feels. Do you want me to leave you alone?"

Alma looked away, chewing her lip. Why had she called Ryan? Why him? Was it *only* because his was the only number she had to hand?

"Tell me honestly, Ryan. The goat in the window. The one that visited me every night for twelve years. Did you put it there?"

Ryan's smile wavered.

"I did not," he said. "I already felt awful for sending you into the room with that dead animal. It was your brother's idea, and I went along with it, and I'm sorry. But I had nothing to do with the head in the window."

"So it wasn't you." Alma let out a jagged sigh. "And my brother was in the attic room, so it couldn't have been him. But there *was* something out there. It's been there ever since. And I'm afraid that it's found me again."

Ryan's gaze was hard to read. What was it behind those eyes? Sympathy? Concern? Pity? He took a long time to consider his answer, and when it came, it wasn't a response she could have guessed.

"*I've* been here ever since. And now *I've* found you again. And I'm telling you that you are not cursed. You don't need your spells, your pendants, or anything else."

He surprised her further by sliding a hand across the table and placing it over hers. She didn't flinch.

"Ryan...?" she looked at his hand and felt a burning on her face.

"Now I'm afraid I have to be going," he said, suddenly releasing her hand and pushing his beer towards her, not even half finished. "I have a parochial council meeting this afternoon and an RCIA group this evening. But tomorrow I have more time. So let me take you out for dinner."

Alma straightened up, pushing her shoulders back to stop her stomach from doing flips. "Are priests allowed to ask women out on dates?"

"It's...not like that."

Alma swallowed. "Not anymore, you mean."

"I'm afraid so. I took my path. You took yours. But I'm allowed to be glad our paths crossed again."

As they left The Academy Bar and Club, Alma wasn't thinking about the shimmering shadows in the street anymore.

Alma knew she had to tell the police about Gerallt, for the same reason she was dialing the number from Robyn's landline: her mobile phone wasn't anywhere in the flat. Supposing Gerallt might have stolen her phone was a long way from suspecting he might have had something to do with the murder. But even if they investigated and found that Gerallt couldn't have been the killer, she might at least get her phone back.

Alma baulked at the notion that Gerallt could have killed that young woman, simply because it made her wonder why she was still alive herself.

She had paced around the sofa enough times to be able to do it with her eyes closed. She focused on the scent of the incense cone burning on the shelf. Robyn was still in bed, and Alma told herself that was the reason she was calling the police without consulting her first. This was a murder enquiry. It was too important.

Had Robyn been asleep all day? Did she even know a woman was dead?

The phone picked up and a man on the other side answered. "Clifford."

"My name's Alma Petrulytė. I gave a statement about the murder this morning."

Clifford's curt tone became suddenly receptive, the musical Welsh accent returning, along with the sound of paper shuffling on a desk. "Of course. How can I help?"

"I need to change the statement I gave."

"I see. Which particular details do you want to change?"

Alma admitted as much as it seemed safe to admit, though none of it was comfortable. She told Clifford about the meeting with Gerallt and his supposed Wiccan Society. Between being in a derelict house which they most likely had no right to be in, and consuming substances that had led to them falling asleep in it, Alma wasn't sure how many potential crimes had been committed. But she admitted to both those things, hoping that volunteering information about a crime scene would be a sufficient counterpoint.

"Right," Clifford said. His tone was cold again. "Thank you for the new information. As it happens, the individual you mention is known to us, so we will follow up on this."

That surprised her. Clifford didn't sound like he had the missing piece of a puzzle to lock up someone they'd long suspected of being a killer. He sounded more like he resented having his time wasted by the kind of person who took drugs from a stranger and fell asleep in a squat.

He told Alma that they might be in touch again and Alma confirmed she understood.

After the call ended, she realised she hadn't asked about her missing phone. It didn't matter. It would have sounded ridiculous after everything else she'd described. Not to mention insensitive, asking a detective in charge of a murder investigation if they could retrieve her phone 'while they were at it'.

It was still only the middle of the afternoon, but in the silent flat she felt ready to sleep again. If Damien had tried to contact her, it would have been on her mobile. Today was Friday. Would he have come to his senses by Monday? Should she bother going into work?

The hunger which was starting to gnaw at her was quickly quashed by the sight and smell of the grease-encrusted kitchen. She made herself the quickest thing she could think of, which was toast with butter. A jar of jam in the fridge was almost full but, when opened, was found to be capped with a pale green film of mould.

Alma closed the fridge door and found herself staring at Robyn's work schedule. No wonder Robyn had chosen to stay in bed: she was due at the hospital at two o'clock the following morning. That meant she probably wouldn't be much company, and Alma would have nothing but time and space to think.

Exactly what she didn't need.

The toast popped. Alma buttered it and took it to her room. It felt oddly safe. She looked out the window to remind herself how little could be seen from it, and how difficult it would be for something else to see back in. She curled her arm up against her chest and stroked her pendants with her fingertips. But she couldn't bring herself to say any words this time. She couldn't make peace with this moment. All she could do was eat, remove her two-day-old clothes, and fall into bed.

Her upper body lashed forwards like a sprung trap. The scream came like a dry, grating banshee's howl. She clutched her throat and heaved for breath, fixing her eyes on the window. Nothing was there but black sky and orange light bleeding around the corner of from the street. Yet she could still see the vacant eyes and bloodied mouth. It had found her. Even here, in her new hiding place.

There was a scampering noise outside the door. Alma turned and lowered her feet to the floor, ready to lunge at whatever came through. Instead, there was a knock.

"Alma? You alright?"

Her shoulders fell, the fight instinct dropping out of her like water from a burst balloon.

"I'm OK. I'm sorry. I was asleep."

Robyn stepped into the room, already dressed for work in maroon scrubs. "You scared the crap out of me. What was that? A dream or something?"

"Yeah, just a dream." Alma said it as though the words would make it true. She felt the eyes watching even now. "Sorry I scared you. Are you heading out?"

"Soon, yeah. How are you feeling after last night?"

"Not too bad. My throat is still scratchy."

"Me too. Have you heard about..." Robyn paused, her mouth hanging open. Alma figured she was reconsidering what might not be a good idea to tell someone who had just woken from a nightmare. So, she lingered purposefully, then asked, "Have you had a message from Damien?"

Alma rubbed the side of her head and feigned grogginess, though she felt like she might never sleep again. "My phone's lost. I don't know."

"Oh. He sent me one saying he'd not heard back from you and that he wants to say sorry. Did something happen at work?"

"I don't know how to explain it. He got angry about something and told me to go home."

107

Robyn's expression seemed to spin like a two-coloured marble: sympathy on one side and outrage on the other. "What an arsehole! What did you do?"

"I met up with Ryan for a drink. Then came home and slept. I'll email Damien in the morning."

Robyn sat down on the end of the bed. "So, your hunky priest pal stepped in to save the day? You think that's just him being a good shepherd?"

"It's him just being a friend," Alma said flatly. "There's nothing more to it than that."

"Is that because it can't be, or because you don't want it to be?"

Alma lifted her gaze to find Robyn staring back at her with mothering eyes. The question was one she'd shuffled to the bottom of the pile a long time ago, never to be asked again. So much about her situation should have made the question stay there, but Robyn was holding it like a magician's punchline.

She said nothing and gave a resigned shrug.

"Will you be seeing him this weekend?" Robyn asked.

"We're supposed to be going for dinner tomorrow."

"His idea?"

"He suggested it."

Robyn rubbed her hands together and then pointed at Alma with finger-guns. "He's trying to get you to lead him into temptation. Priests don't take women out for dinner. Even friends. They invite them to prayer meetings and talk over coffee after Sunday Mass. I'm telling you, Alma, if you want to bag him, you can bag him."

"Oh god," Alma groaned and shook her head. "Robyn, I appreciate what you're trying to do. But it's really…"

Robyn didn't let her finish. "OK fine, if I've got it wrong, I'm sorry. I'll wind my neck in. But if I'm not wrong, just know that I'm going to leave something out for you tomorrow that will help you do what I'm pretty sure you already intend to do."

"Alright, you do that." Alma forced a smile, hoping that Robyn would notice it was time to leave. "Just don't go to too much trouble, because *I* certainly won't."

Robyn got up, grinning to herself, and made for the door. "I'll let you get back to sleep now."

"I'm probably gonna get up and have a shower."

"Ooh, a cold one? Did I already get you hot and bothered thinking about how you're gonna corrupt Reverend Ryan?"

Alma snorted. "No, an extremely hot one because I slept on a floor last night and I feel disgusting. Don't you need to go to work?"

Robyn laughed and left. Alma rummaged around in her bag, pretending to look for shower gel she knew she didn't have, until she heard the main door close, then the gate outside. Robyn was gone. The flat was silent. The middle of the night resumed its true form.

Somewhere out on Penglais Road, she could hear drunken laughter. Students coming down the hill. Had the dead girl been out walking in the dark like that? Would one of those laughing voices out there be next?

No. Alma could still sense the eyes, and they were set solely on her.

She found a plastic shopping bag to stuff her old clothes into, then located a clean towel and made her way to the bathroom. Mercifully, it was much cleaner than the kitchen. Robyn evidently cared more about bathing than cooking, and was more particular about the environment in which she did it.

The shower hissed to life, and a shroud of steam enveloped her. Her world became manageably small. The glass of the shower cubicle misted up, and she became the pragmatic agnostic she had told Ryan she was. She couldn't see what was out there, *ergo* it was not worth worrying about.

It didn't matter how many minutes passed. Each one made her feel cleaner. Yet somehow, there was always something that wouldn't wash off. The water and borrowed shower gel could not remove every trace of the last day.

She turned around to put her face under the spray. There was a dull clunk. Something beneath the shower tray creaked. Alma stopped and strained to listen. She shifted her weight from one foot to the other, trying to make the noise happen again. There was nothing. Then it happened again while she was standing still.

"Robyn?" she called out. Nothing but the rush and pattering of water around her. She waited, holding her breath. The shower was loud in her ears. Would she have heard if Robyn had come into the flat?

Alma directed the shower head towards the tiled wall and opened the cubicle door a crack. The bathroom was thick with steam, but she could make out the shape of the window, the basin, the mirrored cabinet. Turning her head, she saw the door, slightly ajar as she'd left it.

She closed the cubicle door and stepped back under the spray. Under her feet, there was another creak. That had definitely been her; the shower tray was installed unevenly on the floorboards. The air around her turned pale and swirled. She was in no hurry to leave.

Taking the bottle of shower gel, she tried one more time to scrub last night from her skin. Squeezing her eyes closed, she attempted to blink away the sight of that body in the woods. But the memory wouldn't disappear, it only changed. Now the form hanging there did not have a limp covering of blonde hair. It had a long snout, eyes with wide slit pupils and a bloodstained beard underneath its pointed chin.

She scrubbed her skin harder, scraping with her nails until it hurt. Her lips curled back and she hissed, cursing herself. Why was this happening again? How had she failed to defeat this after so long?

The cubicle door flew open. Alma's protective mist gushed away, flowing around a tall figure looming over her. Her mouth fell open, and she looked up at the face she had seen many times. Her nails dug in.

A goat-like face stared down at her, held up by a dark body that was blurred in the fog, clothed in what could have been robes or a long coat. Alma didn't want to scream. She wanted to yell, telling it to kill her if it wasn't going to leave her alone. Her fists balled up, but no other part of her body would move.

The figure lashed an arm towards her. Something hurtled towards her chest. She brought her arms up in time to stop it, but some kind of hard, sharp extrusion scraped her skin painfully. She cried out and stumbled back. Her foot slipped and she fell. Her shoulder bounced off the wall tiles, and she crumpled in the small space.

Frantically, she grasped for something, anything to throw back at the creature. She felt a small, jagged object rolling around under her leg as she tried to right herself. It was the same object she'd been hit with. She gripped it with both hands. It felt like wet hair as she raised it in front of her.

This time, she screamed. She was staring into a pair of brown, hopeful eyes. Flick's jaw hung open, her tongue hanging out daftly. Behind her ears, two goat-like horns had been fixed to the dog's head. That was what had left a scratch on Alma's collar when it hit her.

Consumed by despair and rage, Alma hurled it out of the shower cubicle. The dog's head sailed through the mist and hit the window with a wet thud. There was only empty space in front of her. She heard no creaking of floorboards, nor the opening or closing of doors. But the creature was gone.

Chapter 11

Alma's parents had insisted on moving her bedroom into the side extension of the house, after years of the so-called 'night terrors' waking everyone up. It had become so routine that she always kept pillows bunched at the corner of her bed against the wall, because she knew her first instinct was always to scramble away from the window.

It had been a bad one tonight. Shoulders rising and falling, she did what the counsellor had told her to do, and took stock of everything in her room to ground herself in reality. There was the Sega console, her CD player, the chair with her school uniform draped over the back, ready for the morning.

And there was the dream-catcher hanging in the window, silhouetted by dull yellow light from the street. She'd taken it down once, but her mother reminded her it had been a birthday present and that it would keep her bad dreams away. Three years of evidence had not supported that idea.

A dream catcher couldn't stop something that wasn't a dream. That's what Filip had said.

Alma picked her necklace up from the side table and rubbed it between fingers and palm. She'd added a third pendant to it at the weekend — a moon glyph symbolising 'light' — and now it shifted awkwardly in her hand. She tried a few different ways of holding it until it felt comfortable.

She could hear a fox scratching around by the side of the house, as it often did. Mum had suggested that was what woke her up, but that was stupid. Alma wasn't scared of noises or shadows or animals.

One benefit of sleeping downstairs was easy access to the kitchen without being heard on the stairs. Alma went to the fridge, took out some cheese and began cutting. Eating cheese at night was supposed to give you dreams. It never worked, as much as she hoped for dreams instead of what she had.

The clock on the oven said it was ten minutes to one. There was plenty of the night left. Time enough for the Scapegoat to come to her again. Probably he would wake her just as the sun came up, when it wasn't worth trying to get back to sleep, so she'd read or play video games for half an hour before getting ready for school.

With three slices of cheese and a bread roll on a small plate, Alma switched the light off and returned her room. She stopped in the doorway, then lurched back with a terrified gasp, dropping the plate. It landed with a loud crash that reverberated through the house.

A face was in the window, eyes wide and the mouth moving rapidly. A hand waved towards the door in her room that led outside.

It was Filip. He was supposed to be grounded after he and Bryn were caught vandalising a telephone box up in Llysfaen. Grounded or not, their parents would go ballistic if they knew he'd been out this late.

"Fucksake," Alma hissed quietly as she went to open the door. Filip pushed his way through so hard Alma stumbled. "Where have you been?"

"Fucking nowhere." Filip whirled to face her and jabbed his finger into her neck painfully. "You don't tell

114

anyone you saw me. I was in my room all night. You got that?"

Alma closed the door to get some distance from him, rubbing her throat. "You'd better get upstairs then. I don't care if you get caught or not."

There was a creak from the landing. It was their mother's sleepy, irritable footsteps. Filip was shaking and agitated in a way Alma hadn't often seen. It only happened when her brother knew he was in really bad trouble.

"You fucking should care," he said in a harsh whisper, his eyes flicking from the hall door to Alma and back repeatedly. "He came for me, you know? Like, for real. And this time, he got Bryn."

"What do you mean? What do you mean he 'got' Bryn?"

"I mean Bryn's fucking dead!" Filip's quivering hand shot up to Alma's face. "Scapegoat fucking got him, and he almost got me too. He knows I'm the only thing stopping him from getting to *you*. And that's why you should fucking care if I get caught, because if I'm grounded, I can't protect you."

Alma's breath hitched. It could be difficult to tell when Filip was lying, but there were times when his eyes became haunted orbs and you knew without a doubt he was telling the truth. She began to shake.

"Did he follow you here?" Her voice cracked. "What did he do to Bryn?"

"He came for us both. Got to Bryn first. Pushed him right over…"

"Who's outside? Who's opening the door?" It was mum's voice from the stairs. Filip dropped into a

115

hunched stance like the special ops soldiers in movies.
He inched towards a third door leading to the bathroom.

"Tell her it was you!" Filip mouthed as he quietly
closed the bathroom door and disappeared from sight.

Alma managed to pick up the plate and the food before
her mother appeared in the dining room.

"Sorry," Alma said. "That was me. I didn't mean to be
so loud."

"What in god's name are you going outside for?"

"I heard the fox. I just went outside to look at it."

"Silly girl. It's freezing and you're just in a t-shirt. And
what's that? Were you feeding it?"

Alma produced the plate that she'd been holding down
by her thigh, as if that would conceal it. "No, this was for
me. I dropped it. Sorry I woke you up."

"You'd better not have been feeding it. Bloody vermin.
Go and put that food back. It's not good for you to be
eating in the middle of the night. Waking everybody up.
We moved you down here to put a stop to that!"

Alma tried to move, but something was making her feet
heavy, like invisible manacles. Parents were supposed to
protect you when something was out to get you. Not put
you away out of sight and earshot.

"Sorry." It was a banal apology, utterly empty and
utilitarian. Mum turned and went back upstairs, muttering
and shaking her head. Alma took her plate back to the
kitchen and then got back into bed. She sat upright and in
silence, waiting for Filip to come out of the bathroom,
hoping Mum didn't check his room.

It seemed like a long time went by, but Filip emerged
without a sound, holding his muddy shoes in his hand and

padding across the floor towards the dining room and hall. He stopped next to Alma's bed and leaned over her.

"There are going to be a lot of questions tomorrow," he said grimly. "You have to tell everyone that I was home, in bed. Nobody else believes you about Scapegoat. Only I do."

Alma nodded. She knew.

"And if you tell anyone you saw me," Filip went on, "I might go to prison. Then nothing will stop him from getting to you."

"I won't tell," Alma whispered. She didn't dare so much as turn her head until Filip had left the room.

Then she lay down on her side and looked at the window, past the ineffectual dream catcher. She wasn't afraid to look out the window. She wouldn't see anything there until she closed her eyes.

The next day, there weren't as many questions as she'd expected. She just heard a lot of talk about how one of the boys from her school had been throwing things from the top of the quarry in the night, had fallen and died.

A terrible accident.

Alma stood in front of the phone, shivering and wet with a towel pulled around her. The flat was empty. The front door was closed and undamaged. If she called the police, what would she tell them? What could she say to explain the fact that her new boss' dog's head was in her shower with horns drilled into the skull?

117

No. She walked away from the phone and into the kitchen. There had been little chance to learn where anything was kept yet, so she ignored the smell of grease and opened cupboards and drawers until she found some bin liners.

When she returned to the shower, the amount of blood smeared around the tray shocked her. The head was still there, an oddly shaped, hairy mass with teeth, horns and ragged flesh. She scooped it into a bag, then double bagged it, tied the top three times and pushed it into the kitchen bin, as far as it would go. It didn't feel like a great idea, but she didn't want to risk putting it outside where it could be found or sniffed out by foxes.

She walked back to the bathroom, slowly drying herself. She winced as the towel rubbed her chest. In the mirror, she saw an angry red scrape just below her collarbone. A bruise was starting to bloom on the back of her shoulder. Her eyes looked sunken and dark. Her wet silver hair looked dull and fluid, like brine retreating over a worn pebble.

Do you get what you pray for.

She was still alive, but she hadn't prayed for that. She'd prayed for that woman. She'd even prayed for the dog. Most of all, she'd prayed for Filip. She stared at herself, recalling her brother's voice on the phone and his words. He'd been scared. She had turned him away. Now she was alone, and Filip was…

…she didn't know.

In her room, she got dressed and lay on her bed, over the covers. The view through the window showed the hill, the streetlight, and the moon behind the clouds. She felt illuminated, as though under a microscope.

118

He was still watching her.

Fastening her necklace, she placed a hand over the bunch of pendants. Her eyes were open as she began to speak.

"I cannot make peace with this moment. I don't know if there can be peace anymore. I don't want to be scared anymore. Nobody is keeping you from me. The next time I see you, I want it to be the last time."

Chapter 12

Alma woke without a cry, though it hardly felt like a prayer answered. Her body ached, and she felt as exhausted as if she hadn't slept at all. She made herself eat some breakfast, then took every empty or nearly empty packet she could find and stuffed them into the bin until it was full. She tried not to think about the thing she was hiding.

Her spree continued in the bathroom, scrubbing every last trace of the nightmare from the shower and the vinyl floor. Then she moved on to the kitchen, working as though the moment she stopped someone would knock on the door with difficult questions; like a condemned person digging their own grave, knowing that when the task was done, there remained only to stand at the edge and wait to be shot.

The last job was to empty the kitchen bin. She wrapped it all in an additional liner, put on her jacket and dropped it into the black wheelie bin in the yard on her way out. Stepping through the gate into the street was like returning to the real world from some dark dream land. Beyond the wall around the sheltered yard with its cracked concrete slabs and the shabby bricks, the world was light grey and soft yellow with warm late summer sun. Alma disguised herself with the daylight and walked towards the seafront.

There were more students about town than she remembered of the Saturday mornings during her time in Aber. A group of them filed out of the cafe on Great Darkgate Street. They were laughing, and Alma wondered for a moment if the previous day could have

121

been a dream; that she would see the blonde woman and her friends pointing at her in contempt, mercifully alive. As she got nearer, she *did* see the blonde's face through the window, but it was not a live person. It was on the front page of the Cambrian News being read by an old man. *Police Call for Witnesses after Student Death.* She was smiling and pretty and not at all how she's looked any of the times Alma saw her.

What would happen if no witnesses came forward? Would the police find anything? Did ghosts and devils leave fingerprints? Did detectives have ways to trace curses back to the people who inadvertently cast them? Were the police trying to contact her about her statement right at that moment, either on her lost mobile or on the landline in an empty flat with a dead dog's head in the bin outside?

For a few minutes more, she tried to let the sun flush the chill from her bones. The cries of gulls and shallow, rolling waves sounded like the frayed edges of reality, warning her of the approaching storm of madness. On the frontier of that storm was the *Arcana* shop, with its swirling scents and gloom she was glad to take shelter in. She didn't check to see what the sign on the door said before pushing on it. It opened stiffly and with the jangling of a bell. From behind the counter, a teenage girl with a round face and brown dreadlocks looked up in surprise.

"Oh, that bloody door," she - presumably 'Sara' - said. "We're not open just yet, I'm afraid."

"That's OK," Alma said, taking a sheet of paper from her jacket pocket and laying it out on the counter. Beneath the glass, she could see the *athame* knife display

122

had not been redressed, and there was a prominent gap left by the dagger she'd had put on layaway. "I just wondered if you knew who put this flyer up on your door? I went to the meeting and I think I might have left my phone."

Sara picked the flyer up and took her time reading it.

"There's no phone number on it."

"No, I realise that. Do you remember someone putting it up?"

"I don't, I'm sorry." Sara handed it back and smiled incongruously with her apology. "Who was at the meeting? If you remember their names, I could tell you if they're regular customers."

"I only remember one person," Alma said vaguely. "A black guy called Gerallt. Does he ever come in here?"

"Oh, Gerallt!" Sara beamed and nodded. "I know him. Well, I know *of* him. He's quite a character. I can definitely imagine him being into this sort of thing, but he hasn't been into this shop in a long time. More than a year. Dewi says he's a bit dodgy, and told him he's not welcome."

"You don't suppose he could have come in and put it up without anyone seeing?"

"I wouldn't have thought so. That bell's pretty loud. Wouldn't be easy for someone to come in without being heard."

Alma wasn't convinced of that, but could see that she wasn't going to learn anything more from this girl. It had been a long shot, in any case. She thanked Sara for her help, then tried to buy a box of Persian Musk incense sticks as a token sale for taking up her time. Sara reminded her that the shop was closed and no sales could be made until it was open. Incredulous, Alma apologised and left.

Outside, she found herself once again standing in the sun on the ragged precipice of madness. Dog walkers patrolled the beach. The promenade was empty of cars or people. A spilled kebab and a puddle of dried vomit remained as evidence of the revellers who would have been coming back this way from the *Pier Pressure* nightclub in the early hours of the morning.

To her left, the hill ran up to the crumbling stone chapel, which was illuminated in soft golden light. As soon as she laid eyes on it, she felt like she was being watched. It wasn't just that it was high up; she'd had that feeling so many times before when there was no high ground for someone to be watching from.

From the road, she could just about see the sheer cliff a short distance beyond the chapel. She approached the hill path, fidgeting with her pendants.

She remembered Filip's friend, Bryn — and that Scapegoat liked to push people from high places.

The chapel had sturdy doors at the front and back, both closed and certainly not as old as the walls. No lights came from inside. That shouldn't have been a surprise, but she found in her subconscience a thought that Ryan might have been in there, thinking. Hiding from people and not being interrupted by God.

Nearby was a group of five young boys wearing shorts and t-shirts. Two of them were wet, and Alma thought they must be freezing. Though the sun was warm, a bracing gust swirled over the hill from the sea. She stood near the chapel and watched as one of them faced the cliff edge, took a few steps back, then ran, jumped, and disappeared from view. Alma's stomach flipped, but after a couple of seconds, there was a splash and a cheer from the other boys.

"Hey," she called out, moving closer and folding her arms like a stern teacher. "You shouldn't be doing that, you know. I knew a boy from school who broke his back from tombstoning."

The boys looked at her like she was stupid. One of them laughed and pointed back at the chapel, then at the cliff edge.

"It's fine," he said. "As long as you line up with the door and the flat bit there, the water's always deep enough."

To make his point, the boy took a run and leapt over the edge. Alma closed her eyes and grimaced until she heard another splash and a cheer. When she opened her eyes, the next boy was already lining himself up.

"Just be careful," she sighed. "It only has to go wrong once."

A strong gust scattered her hair into her face. The boys didn't seem bothered by the wind, and watching them was making her feel cold to the bone. She turned and peered through the window of the chapel, just to be sure. If anybody was in there, they were sitting in near-total darkness.

Walking down the hill, she looked at the promenade and the streets running inland from it. She imagined watching someone leave the Arcana store and walk around the corner towards the quay, just as she had two days earlier. Could Filip have been watching her from up here when he called her?

The wind jostled past her, batting in the way that was always louder through a microphone. There had been no wind in the background wherever Filip called her from. He couldn't have been here.

Alma quickly warmed once she was back on the street. She decided to take all of her remaining cash out at a machine so she could monitor spending it carefully. It was just over eighty pounds. She folded a twenty-pound note and put it into her left pocket to ensure she could pay her way at dinner tonight with Ryan. The rest went into her right pocket, to last, by some miracle, until payday.

She went home via the budget supermarket. The name had changed since her time, but it was still very much the same place where she and her housemates had bought frozen meals and party packs of Boddington's beer. As she wandered the aisles, she tried not to imagine what her younger self would have thought to see her at thirty years old, still comparing the price-per-hundred-grams of different packs of pasta and cous-cous.

Still trying to outrun the staring eyes.

With two plastic bags and enough food to eat miserably for a couple of weeks, Alma made her way back to the flat. As she fumbled her way through the gate, she held her breath to avoid inhaling the stench from the bins, which was probably only in her head anyway. She opened the front door quietly and crept inside. Robyn's door was closed: she was probably in there, sleeping after her shift at the hospital, hopefully unaware of anything that had happened since she'd left.

Alma put the food away, listening to the silence in the flat. She thought about the creaking sounds she'd heard in the night, just before Scapegoat had appeared in a way he never had before. She wondered if she ought to check on her new flatmate.

Robyn ought to be safe: she hadn't been named in Alma's prayer.

Alma put an ear to the bedroom door. Someone was breathing slowly and heavily. Asleep. Alive. Alma tipped her head and sighed in relief.

She crossed the narrow hall to her room…to do what? Wait? Keep vigil? Watch to make sure *he* didn't come back?

She turned and closed the door…then lurched back at the sight of a dark shape. Her body tensed, fists clenched, ready to lunge. But before she could build up the momentum to throw a punch, she realised nobody was there. The shape that had startled her was a green satin dress on a clothes hanger.

She released a breath and sat on her bed. Her hand landed on something that crinkled, and she looked down to see a note.

The place looks amazing! Thank you so much for cleaning up. I will try not to let it become a pigsty again. I told you I'd leave something out to help you with your hot priest situation. Doesn't fit me anymore, but I reckon you'll look a snack in it. Promise me you'll save him from his vow of celibacy. You don't need spells or love potions. Never underestimate the power of cleavage. Also, I've left my old phone charging in the lounge. It's a bit shit but it'll do until you find yours. Robyn.

Alma swallowed an embarrassed laugh. The last time she'd worn anything remotely like the dress was the May Ball in her final year at the university, and then only grudgingly. She had to admit it was 'different' enough for her to not completely hate it. But if she was laughing at the content of the note as though it were banter, why was she entertaining the idea of actually trying it on?

Avoiding the thought, she hurried out again in search of the phone Robyn had left. It didn't look all that old, and at least it didn't have an enormous crack across the screen.

She noticed the plates were still on the steamer trunk coffee table from their meal the night before last. Apparently, her cleaning frenzy hadn't made it as far as this room. She hadn't been into the lounge yesterday at all, except to look for her phone. The heavy odour of weed underlaid the lighter smell of incense, but in between there was something else. Something in her imagination, perhaps. There was so much she'd tried to believe was just in her imagination.

Do you get what you pray for? She still didn't know how to answer that. That night with Gerallt was hazy, yet she remembered her words exactly. She remembered the grin on his face and the weight that lifted from her heart as she invoked a blessing instead of a curse. An invocation that had brought death.

So was it a rhetorical question?

The first number she entered into the phone was Detective Inspector Clifford's. She pretended she was calling just to let him know about the new phone number she could be reached on. He asked her what had happened to her other phone, and she seized the opportunity to ask the question she'd really called about.

"I think that Gerallt bloke might have taken it," she said. "Have you caught up with him at all?"

Clifford was surprisingly casual in his reply. "We have spoken with Mr Jones, and he's been eliminated from our enquiries as regards Miss Warwick's death. If you think Mr Jones has stolen your phone, I can put you through to…"

"So you're sure it couldn't have been him who killed her?"

"We've spoken with a witness who has placed him in a different location at the time of death."

"A witness? Who? How do you know they're telling the truth?"

"That's not information I can disclose," Clifford said through a beleaguered sigh. "Unless you have any other information about Mr Jones' activities that night or that morning…"

He paused to give her an opportunity to either share something he didn't know, or figure out for herself that the conversation was over. Alma apologised — she wasn't sure what for — and ended the call.

Gerallt wasn't the killer. Alma stood in silence, wondering how that made her feel. Did she feel anything? Maybe she'd hoped that if it was Gerallt who had killed the woman, that would have at least been a rational explanation. But it was unlikely Gerallt had decapitated Flick and mounted her body to the office wall. Even less likely that he'd broken into the flat, leaving no trace and attacked Alma with the severed head in the shower.

Somehow, Clifford's words had a finality to them. Gerallt was no longer a factor, but last night's attacker still was. After so many years, and in a more real way than ever.

Two phone numbers were all she had. She thought of the people she might have called if she had her own phone. Friends in Anglesea, Wrexham, Manchester. People she could contact even now through social media if she needed. But what would she tell them? Even those she'd stood under the moon chanting spells and incantations with. Who of them would believe that Scapegoat — the figure they'd all charitably, if not sincerely, agreed was not just a recurring nightmare of a childhood trauma, but an oppressive spirit — was now manifesting physically?

Appearing in her home.

Killing people.

Filip would believe her. But running from him was the reason she was in Aberystwyth to begin with. He was one of the people she'd named to the spirit, and now she had no way of contacting him.

Which left one person in the entire world who might still believe her. She entered Ryan's number into the phone, but didn't call, afraid that her continued consideration of Robyn's note might show through in her voice. Instead, she sent a text message, informing him of the new number and asking if they were 'still on for tonight'.

She didn't feel at all hungry, but cooking some pasta provided a semblance of normality that would look convincing if Robyn happened to get up. It was a motion that required almost no thought. By the time Alma realised how far her mind had wandered, the pasta was so soft in the pan it was falling apart. The *fusilli* spirals practically flattened under their own sodden weight when she spooned them into a bowl.

The phone chimed with a message from Ryan. He had meetings until three, but would she like to meet for a couple of pre-meal drinks at four? She heard the message in his voice, and it made her picture him, though in her mind, he wasn't wearing a dog collar. It was the voice of Ryan before he was a priest. Before he was even a man. She didn't hear the irritating haughtiness of the eighteen-year-old who'd boldly asked strangers on the street if they'd invited Christ into their lives. Instead, she heard the gentle, timid fifteen-year-old who'd asked her out to the cinema, and endearingly asked if it could just be the two of them, without Filip.

But this time there was no timidity from Ryan, and there was definitely no Filip.

She quickly tapped out a short reply, saying that was a good time for her. It wasn't until she'd already sent it she realised her muscle-memory had put two kisses after the message. She frowned and hoped familiarity would keep him from noticing them.

The sound of Robyn turning in her bed was audible in the stark silence. Alma returned to her own room and closed the door. The dress hung there like a fairy godmother, waiting to prepare Cinderella for the ball. All it needed was Robyn's face at the top of it, smirking knowingly and waving a starry wand.

Alma tried playing out the scene in her mind, in which she put the dress on and went out hoping to meet a grown version of that gentle fifteen-year-old boy. What if the similarity was an illusion? What if she was like one of the boys on the cliff, putting too much trust in familiarity and repeatability? Would she regret ignoring all the things that had changed?

Would she be dashed on the rocks?

She reached out and stroked the fabric of the dress. The satin felt cold and thin. Putting it on would feel like laying herself bare, as vulnerable as she had been when Scapegoat had attacked her last night.

She couldn't feel like that tonight.

There were more sounds from Robyn's room. She would be awake soon; awake and full of questions and innuendo. Alma quietly slipped her laptop into a messenger bag, then put her coat and boots on. She left the dress hanging on the door and put the note on the bed where she'd found it, hoping it might look as though she'd not been into her room. Then she crept out the front door.

Chapter 13

In the common room of the Old College, a laptop was the most effective disguise. It was the easiest thing to sit down and blend into the meadow of students mounted on uncomfortable circular wooden chairs, eyes down and a cheek resting on one hand. Every once in a while, someone would make themselves conspicuous by getting up to buy something from the vending machines next to the entrance. In the high vaulted ceiling of the former library — the shelves now peculiarly devoid of books, giving the appearance of a severe sort of decorative panelling — amplified the reverberation of every footstep.

Nobody took notice of Alma as she returned to her desk with her third coffee from the vending machine. A message had appeared in her email inbox from Damien, but Alma was too anxious to read it now. It could wait until tomorrow night. By then, she would *need* to know if Damien even wanted her to turn up on Monday. She thought about the contents of the bin outside her flat, and shuddered.

She immersed herself in the cloud documents Damien had directed her to read. Her predecessor had a flowery way of writing which Alma wouldn't be able to emulate. She could only hope that her more pragmatic, to-the-point style was acceptable. Now and then, she found herself wondering how such an iconoclastic atheist as Damien had taken an interest in the subject of art in religion. He reminded her of a postgrad student in Manchester who had bizarrely described himself as a 'renowned theologian' on his CV, all because he was part of the debating society, with a speciality in humiliating born-again Christians.

Paper after paper about how art had been used to communicate ideas in various religious traditions. There didn't seem to be much of a focus on 'why', which was the question that had always interested Alma. Although as she thought about it, it somehow interested her less. Perhaps the last person to hold her job had ignored it precisely because it was obvious.

Perhaps it was as simple as the fact that things are easier to believe in if you can see them, even if that means drawing them yourself. Perhaps there wasn't so much difference between a smiling Buddha and Tom Hanks' basketball companion in the movie Castaway.

Only two days ago, she'd retained a distant hope that she might not have to believe in the goat-faced spirit which had, until then, only manifested in her sleep. Now, she had seen him, undeniably corporeal. Sometimes, when she shifted weight from one arm to the other, her shirt rubbed against the graze on her chest, reminding her how real it had been.

Her eyes flicked to the time, as they had done every ten minutes or so the entire time she'd been there. It was quarter to four — the time she'd decided it was best to pack up. She stood and looked around at the book-less shelves, and all the students who could probably have been doing what they were doing just as easily in their rooms. A library should have been the perfect place to come and think. Instead, it was void, no emptier for her departing than for her arriving.

The sun had rolled across the bay and behind the hill. The chapel now stared darkly down with the light at its back. Anybody up there would see the town swathed in grey and carved with deep shadows. Alma walked towards it, keeping it in view until she turned past the long Gothic college building and back towards town.

Ryan had suggested meeting at Rummers Wine Bar. Eight years ago, it had been famous for serving home-made jelly-baby flavoured vodka. In recent years, it had apparently restyled itself into a nautical-themed gastro-pub. The rafters had been exposed, the bar was cladded in reclaimed driftwood and natural stone, and seafaring artefacts evoked the kind of smugglers' den the building had never been.

Alma was ten minutes late, having underestimated the walk from the seafront to the dock side of town. A few couples and groups were eating meals off slate tiles. There was no sign of Ryan, so she went to the bar and ordered a beer. Though she nursed it slowly, Ryan had still not appeared when it was empty. She took out her phone, wondering if she ought to call him. Did priests get unexpected emergencies they had to attend? Last rites for the sick? Hearing the confessions of a parishioner in crisis? She imagined Ned Flanders from The Simpsons, with his guilt-ridden midnight phone calls to Reverend Lovejoy about some innocuous perceived transgression. The beer had relaxed her enough to permit a small chuckle.

In the corner of her eye, she noticed someone coming directly towards her. She turned and rose, and immediately regretted it when confronted with a student-age woman. She had plump cheeks and copper hair in broad curls that bounced like a cluster of springs as she walked, and she was holding a bundle of pamphlets.

"Hey there, howya doin'?" the woman said in a nasal voice with a wide Canadian accent. "My name's Louisa. I just wanted to find out from you there if you were planning to attend any special events over Halloween, or observe in any way."

Alma recognised the obtuse style of questioning immediately and decided to give Louisa the answer every religious do-gooder hoped for. "Actually, yes. I'll be celebrating Samhain with my coven. I don't like all the commercial rubbish. I go for the real deal."

Louisa's face quickly melted into the kind of expression a GP might make when a patient divulges some particularly embarrassing symptom: a kind of reassuring empathy mixed with the call-to-action attention to someone with a genuine problem.

"It's great to hear that you're seeking something *real* instead of superficial and fake. But did you know that ever since the beginning of time, Satan's main focus has been to divert human hearts away from worship of the true God? He entices humans with the suggestions of power, self-realisation, and spiritual enlightenment apart from submission to the Lord God. Witchcraft is one branch of this enticement."

"Really?" Alma said sardonically, playing the game. "Does it say that in the Bible anywhere?"

"It sure does." Louisa became even more animated, her voice rising and plunging like a theremin instrument. "In Revelation twenty-two, it mentioned witches as people who won't inherit eternal life. *Outside are the dogs, those who practice magic arts, the sexually immoral, the murderers, the idolaters and everyone who loves and practices falsehood.*"

136

Alma formed her mouth into a surprised 'O'. "I didn't know that. What do you think I should do?"

Louisa was practically falling over herself with excitement now. Alma glanced off and noticed a young man attempting to engage one of the bar staff in a similar conversation.

"You should definitely come along to one of our worship meetings," Louisa said, thrusting a pamphlet towards Alma. It featured a photo of a man playing an electric guitar with a rapturous expression. "You're already looking for answers to the bigger questions, so you're halfway there. But any practice that dabbles in a power source other than Jesus Christ is witchcraft. Most people don't know how easy it is to invite the devil into your life without even being aware of it."

Alma's composure faltered. She'd heard this yarn many times before, and felt no more inclination to hang out with a bunch of charismatic evangelicals than she ever had. Yet, in an unwelcome way, Louisa's choice of words managed to dig beneath Alma's skin.

"Maybe." Alma put the pamphlet on the bar, then plucked her necklace out of her shirt and let the pendants hang over the material. "I've got quite a few religions to keep up with already. Anyway, I can't talk long. I have a date with a Catholic priest."

The flurry of blows twisted Louisa's smile into a battered grimace. The last punch seemed to hit the hardest: evangelical types like Louisa often had more vitriol for Catholics than for devil-worshippers.

"I'll pray for you," was the last thing the no-longer-cheery woman said before walking off to see how her companion was doing.

Alma ordered another drink and thought about Louisa's list of the damned. Practitioners of magic. The sexually immoral. It was as though the redhead had been speaking to Gerallt about what had happened the night before last.

Even dogs. Poor Flick.

Murderers. How strange they should appear on a list of sins one could supposedly fall into without realising.

Or was it strange? *How easy it is to invite the devil into your life without even being aware of it.*

It was twenty to five when she saw Ryan breeze in through the door. He was more immediately recognisable than before for some reason. As he spotted her and approached, she realised it was because he was wearing a light blue grandad style shirt. The absence of the dog collar made his brown leather jacket seem less incongruous: made *him* seem less incongruous.

"Sorry I'm so late," he said, catching his breath. "I thought I had enough time to freshen up. I was wrong."

"But you did anyway and made me wait."

"I didn't mean..."

"I don't mind," Alma said with a warm smile. "I'm glad you did. You look more like you. What are you drinking?"

"Ah, OK. Just a coke for now thanks."

"Ryan, you suggested us going out. You're not going to be boring are you? Come on, you're not a Methodist. You can have a drink."

Half of Ryan's face lifted like he was trying not to laugh. "I'll have a couple with our food. Are you OK to eat here, or is there somewhere else you'd prefer?"

"Here's fine," Alma said, turning away from him and signalling to the barman. "Two double Pernod and blacks please."

The barman gave her an odd look, but when Alma stared back, he proceeded to prepare the drinks.

"Wow, I haven't had one of those in a while," Ryan said. "Are we pretending we're sixteen again?"

"Could be difficult. This place isn't much like the Dulas Arms."

"No, it isn't. For one thing, everybody seems to be over eighteen."

Two tall glasses appeared on the bar, filled with a liquid that started off dark purple at the top and faded to a putrid greenish brown at the bottom. Alma passed one to Ryan and held the other up.

"To the good old Dulas Youth Club."

Her toast was met, then Ryan guided her to a table next to a window. It looked out over the sandstone bridge spanning the Ystwydd river that spilled into the harbour. The water winked and shimmered like cut crystal in the low autumn sun.

"Here we are," Ryan said. "A table next to a window, in case you get too warm."

Alma surprised herself with a laugh, remembering how her teenage self always picked window seats so she could cool down by leaning a bare arm against the glass, especially whilst flushing warm after alcohol. She was flushing a little red now, from the fact that Ryan remembered all that.

"I'm cold more often than not these days," she said. "Part of getting old, I suppose."

"If you knew the average age of people I tend to hang out with, you'd see how ridiculous it sounds referring to *us* as old."

Alma took the menu card. "I always thought our friendship was underpinned by the amount of ridiculous shit that used to come out of both our mouths."

"You may be right. And maybe nothing ever changed."

"Not true." Alma's smile fell. "We did stop being friends."

Ryan conceded with a nod. "Yes, we did. And I regret that."

"Me too."

Everything on the menu sounded like standard pub fare, but decorated with ostentatious words like 'artisanal' and 'microherbs'. Alma's eyes glazed over the lengthy food descriptions. The prices were harder to ignore. She chose the cheapest main: a pine nut and pumpkin salad. Everything was going to taste like aniseed after drinking Pernod, anyway.

Louisa had apparently run out of souls to save at the bar, and was approaching tables with her colleague. It didn't take long for one of the staff to intervene and ask the pair to leave. Alma watched as the manager refused Louisa's request for permission to leave some leaflets on the bar. As she left, Louisa turned her head and caught Alma looking at her. The fervent redhead's face dropped, as though seeing something irretrievably reprobate and beyond salvation.

"Someone you know?" Ryan asked.

"No, just someone who was trying to save me from the evils of witchcraft."

Ryan's face tightened with a self-awareness that seemed somehow apologetic. "Oh dear. I assume you deflected her proselytising."

"I told her I had a date with Catholic priest."

Ryan's brow jumped up. "I'm sure that did it."

"You'd know." Alma crossed her arms on the table. "That woman is basically *you* fifteen years ago."

"Impossible. I'd never have had the guts to bother people while they were eating."

Alma huffed. "So you're saying that if I'd made sure I was always eating when we saw each other, we might have been able to stay friends?"

Ryan sighed and straightened his back against the chair. "I said I was sorry for how I behaved back then. But it feels like that was a different life. I was hoping we could start fresh."

"We can. But I'm interested to know if it's just going to go the same way again."

"How do you mean?"

"For example, tell me something honestly: does it really not bother you at all that I continued practising all this time, as recently as two nights ago?"

"You are your own person with your own free will. It's your choice what you do and what you choose to believe."

"That would be very charitable of you if I was a stranger who wanted to be left alone. But that's not what I asked."

Ryan looked at the table and considered his words. "I care about you. That means I want to see you experience the best life has to offer. Now, I'm no longer so quick to see evil in things I don't agree with. However, I have

141

done a lot of community work with people who got caught up in the occult, and I've seen enough to believe that it can have negative consequences."

"What kind of consequences?"

"Anxiety. Depression. Disassociation. Drug dependency. The kinds of things common in people who become reliant on *anything* that promises much, then fails to deliver."

Ryan's list was not like Louisa's catalogue of the damned, but it similarly struck Alma a little too squarely in the chest. She imagined him doing the sort of care in the community work which no doubt came with his job.

Was that how he saw her now?

"It's funny how things can look different depending on which side of the fence you're on," she said. "A lot of the people I used to know turned to white magic for *help* with those exact sorts of things, after being let down by therapy, medicine and organised religion."

"Did they get the results they hoped for?"

"It gave some of us a sense of control over our lives and destinies, so yes, I'd say so."

"Does it help *you* feel happy? Safe?"

If only he'd said *did it* rather than *does it*, she would have been able to answer confidently.

"I don't know." She sipped her drink and winced at the liquorice bite of the Pernod, no longer softened by nostalgia. "I don't suppose you've ever ministered to a guy called Gerallt, have you?"

"Actually, I know just the person you mean." Ryan answered so casually that Alma froze in surprise. "He's been coming to see me for a long time. I don't know how much good it does him. He's a troubled individual."

142

"When was the last time you saw him?"

"Only yesterday. It was very unusual. He came to the presbytery very early in the morning, saying he needed me to hear his confession urgently."

Alma felt cold tendrils curl around her limbs. "What did he need to confess?"

"You know I can't divulge that. What I *can* say — because it's public knowledge — is that he is a sex offender who frequently relapses into unhealthy behaviours, and that he's not someone I would recommend associating with."

Alma folded her arms tightly around herself, one hand instinctively rising to her pendants. Her throat felt tight and dry. "Ryan, you have to tell me...did Gerallt kill that woman?"

"No." Ryan shook his head earnestly. "And that was an example of providence in itself. You see, Gerallt is one of those people who confesses on a Saturday so that he can do it all again on a Sunday. Only God knows how sincere and enduring his confession to me yesterday was. But what is certain is that if he had not been with me at the time he was, he may have become a suspect in that case."

Alma narrowed her eyes and parted her lips as a realisation formed. "You were his alibi?"

"You make it sound like I'm protecting him," Ryan said with a nervous laugh. "The police asked him where he was at the time the woman died. He told the police he was with me, which he was. The police came and asked me to confirm it, so I did."

Once again, Alma experienced mixed emotions knowing Gerallt wasn't the killer, although knowing his background sent a chill through her, considering her own

143

experience with him. The icy claws raking at her insides now belonged to another question entirely.

"So if he wasn't confessing to murder," she asked softly, "presumably he was telling you about other things which had happened that night."

"I'm sacramentally forbidden to share anything he told me."

"You told me he's a sex offender."

"Because it's widely known."

"So you're allowed to tell people if he's confessed to things they already know about."

"No, that's not quite what I…"

"Ryan," Alma said, her voice tense. "What did he tell you about last night?"

Ryan sighed and shook his head. "Everything. I'm sorry, I wasn't going to bring it up. I already told you, it's not my business to judge."

Alma's face dropped into her hands, burning fiercely. "Oh god….what the fuck must you think of me…" She squeezed her eyes closed and gritted her teeth as though it could make her invisible. The next thing she was aware of was his gentle touch on her arm.

"This doesn't change anything," he said. "Look, I'm your friend. If I'd had any inkling you might have crossed paths with Gerallt, I would have absolutely warned you about him. And when I realised you'd been in the same area where there had been a…" He stopped and squeezed her forearm until she lifted her face. "I'm just glad you're safe."

The way he looked at her was like some sort of magic trick. Like he's taken all the sentiments which had driven her away from him years ago, and built them into a place she felt she could run from danger.

"I'm not sure how safe I am."

"What do you mean?"

"He came into my flat last night."

Ryan's expression flattened. "Gerallt came to your flat?"

"No. Not him."

"Then who?"

"You were the one who used to tell me that magic and witchcraft opened the door to evil things."

"I was..." Ryan grimaced uncomfortably. "...Alma, I was a zealous evangelical. I was just spouting the things I'd heard."

"What if you were right?"

"I don't understand what you're saying. Who came into your flat?"

Alma leaned towards him on her arms. "Filip always told me the goat in the window was a devil that would come for me if I didn't allow him to protect me. What if he was right?"

"Has Filip..." Ryan begun, before stopping and looking at her with sudden understanding. "Are you talking about Scapegoat?"

"I know how this sounds, Ryan. But he was in my flat last night. He was there. For real."

"Alma, listen to me. You spent years of your life believing that this creature was coming for you in the night. You've had a traumatic experience. It makes perfect sense that some of those old anxieties might start coming..."

Alma scowled and pulled down the neck of her shirt enough to reveal the red mark where the horn had struck her. "Does this look like a 'traumatic experience' to you?"

"Ouch, that's a nasty scrape. How did it happen?"

"He attacked me. Physically. He was there. I wasn't dreaming."

"You *always* insisted he wasn't a dream."

"Ryan!" Alma's voice rose over the background chatter, and one or two people glanced over. She bit her lip and rested her hand by her face to hide it from the rest of the room. "Ryan, you of all people should understand. You believe in angels and demons and all that stuff. Please. I need you to believe me about this."

Ryan exhaled slowly. "OK. You're right. I believe in good and evil. I believe there are forces we can't see, even here on earth. But I also believe in fear, and the power it can hold over the human mind."

Alma shook her head in exasperation. "Don't try to convince me this is all in my head."

"I'm not trying to convince you of anything." Ryan's hand landed on hers and closed around it with a surprising grip. "I'm telling you that I am looking at someone I care about who is very scared. That's all I need to understand to know I want to help."

For a moment, Alma just stared at his hand. She recalled a time when they'd been sitting opposite each other just like this, in some greasy spoon cafe in Llandudno or Rhyl or somewhere. She'd watched his trembling hand drift back and forth across the grey laminated table as they talked, sometimes passing close to hers before bottling out and retreating. Now, his hand enveloped hers without hesitation, like a blanket thrown over someone pulled from the sea.

"You don't believe he's real though," she said weakly.

"I don't need to decide that now. But I promise I'll help you face this, whatever it means and whatever it takes."

Chapter 14

The town centre was lively as they made their way back. Alma read the names of all the places she remembered. It used to be said that there were fifty-two pubs and clubs in Aberystwyth; one for each week of the year. In the square, gangs of first-year students were being led on their inaugural pub crawls.

The clear skies which had made for a warm day also made for a bracingly cool evening. Alma thrust her stiff hands into her jacket pockets and nodded towards the coat-less freshers, most likely regretting their choice of outfits: girls in short dresses and boys in muscle-fit shirts.

"Maybe it's like you said earlier," Ryan said. "You only start to feel the cold when you're older."

Alma smiled and hurried through the square. Music throbbed from Academy, where she'd had coffee with Ryan the day before. They walked past the 'Why Not' bar and lounge, which was new to Alma. A man in a polo shirt bearing the name of one of the campus blocks briefed a small crowd of freshers in pub-golf outfits.

The man looked over at Alma and raised his hand. She wondered for a moment whether she recognised him. Then, Ryan raised a hand in return and the man shouted, "Evenin' Father!"

"I wouldn't have taken him for a churchgoer," Alma said. The man pointed at them whilst saying something to three girls in pleated mini skirts, who laughed at whatever the joke was. "Another 'confess today and do it all again tomorrow' type?"

"I'm on the university chaplaincy team. Most of the union representatives know me."

Alma laughed. "So finally it makes sense. Being a priest in a university town means you get unfettered access to any young women in need of spiritual guidance."

"Not true," Ryan said, feigning hurt. "It's the men too."

The jacket wasn't quite enough to keep the chill out, so Alma removed her hands from the pockets and wrapped her arms around herself. They left the square and started up the hill. Occasional bands of student stragglers passed them going the other way.

"This isn't on your way at all," Alma said. "The flat's not too much further. You don't have to…"

"It's fine. I could do with walking it off. Unless you'd rather I…?"

"No, no…" Alma wondered whether he meant 'walking off' the modest meal or the several subsequent drinks they'd had. The noise of town receded, and an uneasy hush set in as they suddenly seemed to have nothing to say. She flicked her gaze down to see if Ryan's hand would be at his side, drifting next to hers, waiting. But his arms were folded around himself, just like her.

"What is Filip up to these days?" Ryan asked eventually. Alma's shoulders became heavy and tense.

"I'm not really sure. He was three months into a four-year prison sentence for aggravated burglary, but he escaped and now nobody knows where he is."

"He escaped? How did he manage that?"

Alma screwed her nose up at the question. "I've no idea, Ryan. You know what Filip was like. Clever. Quick. Manipulative. Good at getting away with things."

150

Ryan huffed through his nose and looked down at the pavement, a momentary wash of bitterness showing on his face.

"I can't imagine it's an easy thing to do, escaping from prison. Much harder than creeping down from an attic room and back up without being noticed."

Alma knew he was right. She waited until a drunk trio of young men in togas passed them by.

"I never really believed it was you who did that, you know," she said.

"It doesn't matter. I already got the beating for it."

"I'm sorry for that. You know I hated the way your father was with you."

"We both had overbearing fathers. Neither of us had it easy."

"I know." Alma inched closer and let her arms fall to her sides. "And I know that's why you were always trying to look out for me. You were the big brother I should have had instead of Filip."

Ryan's face scrunched into a pained smile. "You wish I'd been your brother?"

Alma felt her cheeks burn. "No."

The tattoo parlour came into view. A light was on inside for the first time Alma had seen. She stopped at the gate leading to the yard. No lights were on in the flat. Was Robyn working? Or just out? Or sleeping?

"This is the place," she said. "Can I offer you a coffee before you walk back?"

Ryan hunched his shoulders and forced a polite smile. "I...can't...you know…"

"Sorry, I didn't mean anything like that," Alma lied, knowing full well that it was too late for coffee and she

151

didn't even know where the coffee was kept. "I just thought you might like to see where I'm staying."

He nodded awkwardly, and Alma almost regretted trying to persuade him. The regret only increased as she led him past the wheelie bins inside the yard, trying not to let her gaze be pulled towards them. Her heart was racing, and not in a pleasant way. She led him up to the front door and took a little too long searching her pockets for the key. When she found it, she laughed apologetically and looked at him. There wasn't much light in the porch, but she could see he'd gone sickly pale. He was staring at the front door, as though he'd just caught a whiff of some unbearable stench and was flinching to get away.

"Are you alright?" Alma asked.

"I— I shouldn't be doing this," Ryan stammered. "I know it's innocent and everything, but… if someone saw… It's not responsible of me. It's really late too. I should just head off."

"Oh, OK, if you're sure." Alma nodded vigorously, shaking off her disappointment. "I haven't upset you, have I?"

"No, I'm fine, honestly." Colour returned to Ryan's face. He smiled brightly and placed a hand on her arm. "Sorry, I'm making too big a deal of this. It's been great seeing you again. Let's make plans again soon."

Alma promised they would, stepped inside, switched the hall light on and turned to see him off. She waited until the creaking of the steps outside faded away, then she switched the light back off and plunged herself into darkness.

The flat was silent. Nothing, not even snoring or breathing, could be heard at Robyn's door. Alma went into the kitchen and started searching for the coffee, wondering how quickly her lie would have been uncovered if Ryan had accepted her invitation. It didn't take long to find a jar of mostly congealed instant granules. The kitchen was cold. She made a cup of black coffee, just for an aroma to focus on and something warm to hold in her hands.

Something creaked in the hallway. Alma leaned back to look through the open door. Nothing had changed. It was still empty and dark. Raucous laughter came distantly through the kitchen window. More students heading down the hill.

"Robyn?" she called out. Hissing a curse under her breath when there was no answer, Alma pulled open a drawer and took out the biggest knife she saw. "I swear to god, if anyone's there, you're going to get stabbed."

Nothing. She stared at the front door a moment longer. The rickety porch outside cast so many irregular shadows that it would be difficult to tell if someone was standing outside.

Alma left the kitchen with her mug and her knife. The bathroom door was open, and the lounge door was ajar. She stopped at the sound of another creak. It was impossible to locate, as though it were underneath the floor. The kind of sound one would normally dismiss as 'house noises'.

She clenched her teeth and nudged the lounge door with her arm. The floorboards made a distinctly different noise under her feet. She had no reason to suppose anyone was in the flat. *Except for the fact that there had been the night before...*

The lounge was dark, except for a pallid glow from the streetlight behind the drawn curtains. The smell of the coffee mixed with the lingering incense and weed to create something acerbic and coppery. There was a blanket on the sofa and an empty microwave meal dish on the arm, next to the TV remote. Gripping the knife, Alma placed her mug on the steamer trunk in the middle of the room and turned back to switch on the light.

Satisfied the room was empty, she swatted the door shut behind her. It didn't swing as fast as she expected; it felt heavy. Alma turned to push it closed. As soon as she saw the blood streaked humanoid shape, she yelled and brought her knife up.

Robyn's pale, naked form was unmoving, apart from the slow drift of the door. Her arms were raised, nailed through the wrists into the thin, fragile wood which was already starting to rupture under the weight of the body. Dead eyes were rolled up towards the ceiling, a stream of red streaking down the middle of her torso from the small slit in her throat.

"No! Fuck you!" Alma cried out, filling the air with grief and rage.

The elusive creaking sound came again. Alma spun around on the spot, brandishing the knife and ready to lunge at anything that moved. Seeing nothing, she pulled at the door and lurched into the hall, looking for the robed figure which had been so bold to come near when she'd been unarmed in the shower. Her arm shook with the desperate need to lash out, but she found no target.

The front door rattled. Alma jolted back. The amorphous shadows on the window were moving now. Somebody was on the other side. She gripped the knife tightly and sucked in a deep breath, trying to re-inhale the fury which seemed to have escaped her lungs. She watched, waiting for something to come bursting through. Her heart drummed so loudly in her ears that she took a few seconds to realise she was ignoring a voice on the other side of the door.

"Alma? Are you alright? Open the door. What's happening?"

She staggered forward, her legs suddenly weak as the unspent fight instinct drained from her. After she opened the door, she hobbled back a couple of steps and leaned against the wall. Ryan stood in the porch, suddenly speechless and staring at her hand, which still brandished the knife.

"It was him," she gasped. "He killed Robyn. She's dead. I told you...I told you he's not a dream anymore."

"Alma," Ryan said calmly, raising his open hands. "It's OK. Is there anyone inside with you now?"

Alma shook her head. "I don't think so."

Tentatively, Ryan stepped over the threshold. His eyes were fixed on hers, though she noticed glances towards the knife in her hand. She lowered it and turned so that her back was flat against the wall.

"Where is Robyn?" Ryan asked.

Alma looked towards the lounge. Ryan skirted around her, the floorboards creaking loudly with each step. He disappeared from view. There was no sound, but a moment later he reappeared, grim-faced and hands clenched.

155

"You're sure there's nobody else in the flat?"

"I don't know."

"I don't think whoever did this would have stayed. It looks like it happened a good few hours ago."

Alma wasn't satisfied. She launched herself at Robyn's bedroom door. It slammed open. The room was empty. She did the same to her own room and found it just as she had left it. Ryan was getting out his phone when she pushed past him to check the bathroom. It was the same. Alma pounded the wall and screamed.

"Where are you? I'm here! Come and get me!"

Her own voice mocked her in shrill reverberations off the tiled walls. When she sensed Ryan in the doorway, she kept her back to him to hide her eyes, clouded with tears of fear and anger.

"It's alright, Alma. There's nobody here. I'm going to call the police. You're going to be safe."

Alma sensed her legs failing. She dropped the knife into the sink, gripped the cold metal of the towel radiator, and allowed her body to melt onto the floor. "Why is he doing this? Why Robyn? Why that student? What does he want?"

Ryan knelt beside her, one hand on her shoulder and the other dialing on his phone. He kept telling her it was going to be OK. He wasn't listening to her questions. He still didn't believe her. The police wouldn't believe her either. She listened motionlessly as Ryan asked for someone to be sent immediately, gave the address and described what he'd found. He repeated several times that there was no danger to anyone at the scene, and Alma suspected that was for her benefit.

But he was wrong. She knew the danger could be anywhere it wanted.

"They'll be here soon," Ryan said. "What do you need? Water? Something hot?"

Alma shook her head. "We can't stay here."

"Of course. Shall we wait for them outside?"

"No, we have to go somewhere else. I can't talk to the police. What am I supposed to say?"

"Just tell them the truth. You haven't done anything wrong."

"No!" Alma laboriously lurched forwards and pushed herself up onto her feet. "All of this has been happening around me, and the only explanation I have is one nobody will believe."

Ryan glanced about thoughtfully. "I didn't tell them it was *you* who found the body. I could take you somewhere safe and come back to deal with the police."

It didn't seem like a good idea. Was there a better one? Alma had no answers to give. The police knew her in connection with the death of another woman. Ryan was the trusted parish priest.

"Where, though? This thing is following me around. I don't want to put anyone else in danger."

"You can stay at the presbytery tonight. I have a guest room. Then tomorrow you can decide what to do."

Alma nodded wordlessly. The impetus to leave the flat breathed strength to her legs, and she started walking. They left the front door open. Putting on her jacket as she descended the steps outside, she instantly felt the eyes on her. Even in the enclosed yard, they seemed to watch from a great distance. She only wished the creature would come out of the shadows again so she could confront it there and then.

"Won't they wonder why you left the scene?" she asked Ryan as they passed through the narrower streets that sloped steeply down and up again.

"Don't worry about that. I'll think of something to say."

Alma was nonplussed at how calm he was. Was dealing with dead bodies, crime scenes and the police a common duty for the Catholic clergy? She didn't want to ask.

Trinity Road was in a tucked away estate close to the train station. The houses here were mostly semis, larger and better kept than the terraces on the north side of Penglais Hill. It was an area Alma had never been to, nor likely anyone who'd lived in Aberystwyth as a student.

The presbytery itself was a detached house set back from the road. It had a gravel courtyard in front of it occupied by one small grey hatchback. Ryan opened the front door for her, and she was immediately smothered by a hot wave of dry, musty air.

"The heating system is really old," he explained. "It's either full blast or nothing at all."

From the outside, the house had seemed absurdly large for one person to live in. Now that Alma was inside, it made a little more sense. The first door she passed in the hallway led into an office. Opposite that room was the cavernous lounge with a dated brown marble fireplace and a nest of comfy chairs and couches arranged for communal gatherings and meetings. What little personality the home had certainly wasn't Ryan's. Even so, the air hung with a sense of detachment, which for the time being Alma found reassuring.

"Which is the guest room?" she asked. "I'll make sure to keep out of the way if you have any people coming and going."

"Nobody's coming here until Monday," Ryan said, leaning into rooms and turning lights on. "I'll be out most of the day myself. Two Sunday morning masses, and then some home visits. You'll have the place to yourself. That's alright, I hope."

Alma nodded and followed him up the stairs to a small room. It looked like it had been dressed by someone's grandmother, with peach coloured walls and soft yellow bedding. There was a stack of cardboard archive boxes at the foot of the bed. A row of ironed shirts hung from the curtain rail. The air was sterile and faintly floral. The window looked out onto a lawn enclosed by hedges, tall wooden fencing, and a large wooden shed. Truly, it felt like a bubble away from the outside world.

"Thank you," she said, folding her jacket on the bed and turning to face Ryan. He was standing in the doorway, a smile forced over his obvious anxiety to get back to the police. "I hope this doesn't cause you any trouble."

"It won't. Why would you think that?"

"It wouldn't be the first time you've suffered the consequences of my troubles."

"Hey, come on," Ryan laughed nervously. He stepped into the room and took her hand. "This isn't anything like that. I can't explain everything that's happening to you, but we're not children anymore. The police can't just punish anyone when they can't figure out who's really guilty."

"But they *won't* find him. He's always just..." She stopped and slowly pulled her hand away. She studied his face and saw weary impatience, but no fear. He seemed to believe his own words. The room became suddenly cold. "He can still find me here. I know it. This was a mistake. I shouldn't have let you do this. What if he..."

"What if he tries to hurt *me*?" Ryan said. "I'm not afraid. If there is something evil following you, then it will not be able to come into this house. Of that I am certain."

Alma felt a twist of equal parts terror and relief. "So you're admitting he could be real?"

Ryan didn't answer. He lifted a hand towards her neck. She reflexively leaned away, as though flinching from someone trying to touch a wound. Ryan's fingertips landed gingerly on her sternum and for a moment she dared not move. Then he lifted the cord around her neck and held the Benedictine Cross, letting the other pendants hang loosely. He closed his eyes and spoke, his voice calm and grounding.

"O God, by whose word all things are sanctified. Pour forth your blessing upon this pendant, that we may use it in your service and for the good of all your people. Amen."

He released the necklace, opened his eyes, and smiled. "If you believe there's evil watching you, then you can believe there's good now watching you, too."

Though wrung out and powerless, Alma couldn't save herself from laughing. She lifted the cross and looked at it, not believing for one second that it was going to

160

protect her from anything. Nevertheless, his assurance made her feel just slightly safer.

Ryan was clearly mindful of the police, who would be at Rheidol Terrace by now. Alma thanked him for everything he'd done and insisted he not tarry any longer. He disappeared, and she heard the sound of the little car on the other side of the house starting up, making a considerable amount of noise on the gravel driveway. She certainly wouldn't fail to hear anybody approaching the house from the front.

She turned to the window and listened to the unfamiliar silence. No traffic or students. A little pocket dimension set apart from the rest. She breathed slowly and imagined the eyes watching, hanging back.

"You really can't get me here, can you?" she whispered. With that, she turned out the light and lay down on the bed. The darkness filled with an uneasy stillness. A peace hung over her. It was held up on one side by the notion that she may truly be on sanctified ground where evil could not tread. On the other side, it was suspended by a deferential acceptance that Scapegoat would be quick to prove if she wasn't.

Chapter 15

Scapegoat's fist rapped the door slowly and continually. Amid the rows of dark windows spanning away to the left, a curtain twitched. He imagined a neighbour behind it, grumbling about the knocking which had been going on for about five minutes. No doubt the people who lived on this road were used to unusual activity at this particular address.

Even his goat mask might not seem noteworthy to them by the standard of the occupant's usual visitors.

The door opened a crack, and Gerallt's bloodshot eyes appeared. His voice sounded like gravel. "Oh, it's you."

It was amusing how Gerallt opened the door and leaned out to see who was watching, as though he had a reputation to protect. When invited in, Scapegoat followed Gerallt into the living room, which was thick with the smell of an unwashed body and burned substances.

"I didn't think I'd be seeing you again so soon," Gerallt said. He tumbled onto a mattress and began to roll a cigarette. "Is there a problem?"

Scapegoat remained near the door. Gerallt was a pitiable sight. His wild dreadlocks looked like a mound of earth he was trying to bury himself under.

"I got what I needed," Scapegoat said. "And I note that you took a little extra payment for yourself."

"The girls?" Gerallt's shoulders bounced, pumping out a deranged chuckle. "Was I not supposed to fuck them? You should have been more specific about that."

Gerallt lit his cigarette and reclined against the wall looking pleased with himself. Scapegoat's mask grinned back at him, but the face beneath it did not.

"How often those who point up are the ones who drag down," he muttered.

"Amen to that," Gerallt said, throwing his arms wide and scattering ash over the mattress. "You know who taught me that first? My vicar. Oh, the things he did to me would make the things I did to those girls look like Sunday school. Except that he usually did them to me *after* Sunday school."

"I'm not interested in your justifications."

"Then why are you here? I've got nothing more to say, and I'm not gonna offer you a fucking cup of tea."

"There's one more thing I need from you."

Gerallt snorted. "Go fuck yourself. I don't need the pigs coming around asking about any more dead people. Our deal is done."

"You won't have to explain anything. It will be easy. I've protected you so far, haven't I?"

"What's in it for me then? You keep bringing pussy like that to my door, maybe we can talk. Otherwise, I'm out."

Scapegoat took two steps forward. Gerallt was not intimidated, and looked like he was only half listening, his eyes sinking into a mire of deep red.

"This will be the last thing I ask of you," Scapegoat said, reaching into a pocket of his long coat. "After tonight, you won't see me again."

"Oh, I don't know. I'm sure we'll find ourselves hanging out together one day." Gerallt was laughing again. He knocked ash from his cigarette and pointed it at the floor. "You know...*down there.*"

164

This time, Scapegoat smiled beneath the mask. "If I'm that unlucky."

The thin curtains and the pastel coloured shirts hanging from the rail filtered little of the morning light. The walls seemed to glow translucent pink, creating a whimsical sense of being small and safe within the bud of a rose. Alma felt strangely light and relaxed. The bed was far too soft, and the radiator gurgled noisily. Yet she had slept soundly and uninterrupted until...what was the time?

She got up and found the phone in her jacket, but it was dead. She listened for a minute, but the rattling radiator was all she could hear. With every movement, she felt her clothes sticking to her. The room was stiflingly warm.

Without thinking twice, she took one of the hanging shirts and helped herself to a shower. The bathroom was tiled in moss green and seemed as little-used as the guest bedroom. Presumably, Ryan had his own en suite and the main bathroom was for whatever overnight guests a priest might expect to have.

As she stood under the spray, she tried to imagine what Ryan might have said to the police to explain why she wasn't there. He'd seemed so confident, like he believed the word of a man of the church was enough. But even if that confident smile could make the police forget to ask where the victim's flatmate was, it didn't change the fact that Robyn was dead. Or that she was dead precisely because Alma had come into her life with a darkness following after her.

A clock at the top of the stairs read half-past eleven. She couldn't remember the last time she'd slept in so late. Wearing Ryan's shirt with yesterday's jeans, Alma took her phone downstairs to look for a plug socket. She wasn't sure what she would need it for yet. Perhaps there would be a message from DS Clifford. It wouldn't take him long to deduce her proximity to the deaths of two women in as many days.

The sofas in the lounge were not a mis-matched set, each looking old and stiff, perhaps designed to keep people from nodding off during parochial parish council meetings. Had Gerallt sat on one of these in the early hours, confessing his sins to Ryan? Telling him everything they'd done. Had Gerallt perhaps even stayed the night in the peach coloured room, or showered in the moss green bathroom?

Alma rubbed her arms and shuddered, and the house was suddenly not such a sanctuary from evil. Her hand went to her neck, fidgeting with her pendants out of habit. They were all bunched together, the profane ones apparently not repelled in any way by the newly blessed Benedictine cross.

A key in the front door gave her a start. She considered hurrying upstairs and sealing herself inside the rose bud room, unanswerable to anyone. Then came the sound of Ryan's voice, singing something quietly to himself as he entered. He appeared in the lounge doorway, dressed fully in black with the white collar across his neck, holding a plastic shopping bag.

"Hey. How are you feeling?" he asked when he saw her.

"I'm OK. Have you been out all night?"

"No, not at all. I was up early for Mass. I got some things for lunch. You hungry?"

"I don't know," Alma said truthfully. Ryan walked past her with the same confounding calmness, and through a door at the other end of the room. Alma frowned and followed him into the kitchen.

"I spoke to a lady this morning who has a room to let," he said. "I put in a good word for you and she said you can move in whenever you're ready."

He'd clearly assumed that Alma wouldn't want to go back to Robyn's flat, and that was probably true. Evidently, he was also keen to move her out of his spare room. That was understandable, if a little hurtful.

"What happened last night?" she asked.

Ryan sighed like he'd been hoping to put off that conversation. "I told them precisely the truth about everything. I said you weren't in a fit state to be interviewed. They will still need to talk to you eventually, but they agreed to let you have the night to recover."

"Just like that?" Alma frowned. "What's happened with Robyn? Did they manage to contact her family or...anybody?"

"I'm afraid I don't know about that. It's all in the police's hands now. There really wasn't all that much for me to do."

Alma watched him unpacking a French loaf and strong-smelling wedge of cheese wrapped in thin paper. She shook her head incredulously. "How do you do it? Find somebody murdered one night, then just get up early, do

167

a church service and swing by the deli for lunch. Doesn't it bother you?"

"Yeah, it bothers me," Ryan said with slightly more force in his voice. "But as tragic as this all is, may God forgive me if I count myself thankful that once again it wasn't *you* who…"

He stopped himself and started slicing the loaf, dragging the knife in abrupt sawing motions. Alma suddenly felt guilty for asking. She spotted a kettle next to the sink and walked over to fill it up.

"I shouldn't have said that. It was ungrateful. You're sticking your neck out for me."

Ryan stopped, leaned with both hands on the counter, and shook his head. "I'm not doing much, but hopefully I'm doing the right thing. Hopefully, I'm helping you more than Filip would be if he were here."

"You've been great," Alma said, turning to the window and furrowing her brow. She put the kettle on to boil and opened cupboards until she found one containing more mugs than one person could use in a week. She didn't want to imagine how Filip would have handled the situation last night. "I am going to have to try to contact him, though," she added.

"Why?" Ryan turned abruptly. "I thought he escaped from jail. You think speaking to him is the best idea?""

"I don't want to see him. I just need to know he's OK."

"OK? He's on the run from the police. I think that's all the answer you…"

Alma whirled up to Ryan, scowling. "Don't tell me what I should think about my brother! I need to know he's alive."

Ryan drew back in surprise. "I'm sure he's alive. Why wouldn't he be? It's only the police who are after him."

"I need to get my old phone back. He called me. The number will still be on it. I need to know. I can't be responsible for him too."

"After all the trouble he caused you, why would you think you are responsible for him?"

Alma released a defeated sigh. Once again, she was in a position where it was her and a priest, and *she* was going to sound like the irrational one.

"When Gerallt held the meeting the other night—" She noticed Ryan fold his arms uncomfortably at the mention of it. "— I prayed a blessing over two people and a dog. Two of those are now dead. That Claire girl, and my boss' dog. The third was Filip."

Ryan sucked in a breath through his teeth. "Alma, I know how it must look. It's terrible what's happened, but I really think…"

"It doesn't matter what you think. I just need to know if you're going to help me or not."

She challenged his gaze as the kettle roared, trying to act like she had more of a choice than she really did. If Ryan refused, she would have to walk out in search of her phone alone. And clearly, that would not look good to DS Clifford.

"Alright," Ryan said eventually. "Of course I will help you. But if you speak to Filip and find out where he is, you have to let the police know. The sooner they get to him, the sooner he can get the help he needs."

"I know," Alma said. A shrill, plain tone of a phone message came from the next room. She wondered if it was her phone or Ryan's.

"When did you lose your old phone?" he asked, eventually.

"At Gerallt's house. I think I left it there, or he took it."

"You're sure?"

"Pretty sure."

"Well, you're probably right." Ryan shrugged.

"Did he mention stealing a phone in his confession?"

"No, but it probably slipped his mind among all the other stuff he was confessing to."

Alma's face burned once again, and she hoped she was only imagining the accusation in his tone. "Would he have sold it?"

"He probably forgot about it and still has it somewhere." Ryan dusted crumbs from his lap and stood. "If you want, I could go and talk to him. I think I could get him to give it back."

"What, just like that?"

"He trusts me. I seem to be able to prick his conscience more than most."

Alma believed that. "I want to come too."

"You think that's a good idea?" Ryan said. Alma fired him a look, and he raised a concessionary hand.

"Good." Alma turned away from him as the kettle clicked. "Where do you keep the coffee?"

Chapter 16

Alma hurried down the stairs, pulling on her jacket and energised by the simple meal they'd eaten off their laps. Ryan was by the front door, ready to go. He pushed his clerical collar against his neck, like a rider checking his helmet was secure. His face was grey and grim, and Alma wondered what ordinary Sunday afternoon activities she was keeping him from. She tugged at her necklace and held up the Benedictine Cross.

"Think we're taking enough protection?"

Ryan smiled. "I'm sure we'll be fine."

His little car was immaculately clean on the inside and had a faint sweet smell, like really cheap perfume. As they pulled noisily off the gravel drive, she looked around for an offending air freshener, but didn't see one. She sniffed the arm of her shirt, but just caught a faint powdery whiff of detergent. Alma preferred to assume that it was a church smell than to imagine how many other women Ryan had been driving around with. She tried to ignore it and turned the radio on to some music to distract her.

"I haven't been listening to the news," Ryan said. "Have you read or seen anything?"

"No, I've not really looked. I don't need to read about it. We saw it for ourselves."

Ryan nodded, as if in approval. "Indeed."

Gerallt's road was as bleak and grey as Alma remembered it. Police tape still crossed the woodland path at the end of the cul-de-sac, though much of it was broken and flapping loose. The derelict house was even uglier in the daylight. Just as when she'd first visited it, it was hard to imagine anyone actually living there.

"Are you going to come in, or..?" Ryan asked as he pulled up, apparently unwilling to suggest outright she might prefer to wait in the car. Alma unclipped her seatbelt and got out, and led the way to the front door.

Her lungs felt tight as she lifted her hand to knock on the door. Coming down this path the first time had been her biggest mistake. What was Gerallt going to be like, seeing her again? Would he be embarrassed and contrite, like the penitent who'd gone running to Father Ryan for confession? Or would he enjoy being reminded...

No answer came from within. Ryan leaned past her and knocked again, slow and confident, less aggressive than she had been. Alma balled her fists, and thought about how much more satisfying it would be to punch Gerallt in the face and walk in to find her phone, than to have Ryan ask politely.

"Looks like he isn't in," Ryan said. "I can try again later when I'm on my way to..."

Alma rejected his offer by leaning back and bracing herself against him, then slamming her foot into the door. There was a sharp screech as the latch sheared through the aluminium frame, and the door clattered against the wall inside. She stepped in and was immediately swamped with the smell of damp and smoke.

"Knock knock," Alma called out. "Don't fancy opening the door? Now that I know what you really are, you piece of shit."

"For heaven's sake, Alma!" Ryan was close behind her, swearing to himself and testing the door to see if it would close again. "Do you really want to add breaking-and-entering to the list of things the police want to talk to you about?"

Alma ignored him. She went directly for the door to the room it had all happened in. It was dark. The boards over the windows afforded no light at all, and no candles were lit. Yet it was the epicentre of the wave of ugly smells and one hideous memory. Her eyes adjusted to the gloom, and she could see the room was unoccupied. Piles of rubbish, clothes and bedding were strewn about. The thought of rummaging through it for her phone made her gag.

She turned and powered out of the room just as Ryan was catching up, having given up on the irreparably broken door. The kitchen was next. She recalled the unfathomable dryness in her throat when she'd been in there trying to get water.

"This could get us both into serious trouble," Ryan protested, following her closely as she made for the stairs. Her foot-falls on the uncarpeted steps reverberated loudly. Two doors at the top were open, the last one was closed. That was the one she threw her weight against, wrenching the handle.

A second later, she threw her hands up defensively at the sight of Gerallt with his hands raised above his head. She reeled away from the attack, colliding with the stair post and sliding along the railing to avoid the incoming blow.

But Gerallt wasn't moving. He was naked, in the middle of a bedroom with his wrists tied to a fixing in the ceiling. His head hung forward, his legs limp. A red streaking running down the middle of his chest made his Green Man tattoo reminiscent of Christ with a crown of thorns. A dark red patch on the bare floorboards beneath him was still shiny and wet.

Her anger was gone. All Alma could do was stare and wonder when this had happened. Suspended by his wrists and stripped down to his skin, Gerallt was a far cry from the beguiling, lean-bodied figure he had been that night. Now, he just looked wiry, withered and dead.

Ryan's footsteps came up behind her, slowing as he reached the top and looked into the room. "No...not another one…"

"I should have realised this would happen," Alma clenched her fists and walked into the bedroom.

"Stop!" Ryan hissed. "Don't touch anything! We can't leave any trace that we were here."

"It's fine," Alma replied flatly. "You were *his* alibi. You can be mine, too."

"This is *not* the same as that, and you know it. We're not supposed to be here at all."

Alma turned on the spot, slowly scanning the room. There was a window facing the woods, which looked out directly onto the woodland path and the police tape flapping in the wind. Next, she faced the wall with the door and the only other feature on the plain, grey plaster walls. A message daubed in blood: *'Do you get what you pray for?'*

Ryan was staring at her from the top of the stairs. She nodded at the wall he couldn't see. "Do you believe me now?"

"What do you mean?" Ryan crept in, glancing at the body and his own feet in turn. When he saw the message, he froze.

"He's been leaving that message for me," Alma said. "Something Gerallt did the other night started all of this."

Ryan's face turned as grey as the walls. "You really think Scapegoat did all this?"

"I don't know what else to believe! He came and attacked me *in the flesh* in Robyn's flat. Everyone who was part of my prayer, or who was there when I said it, has had their throat cut like a slaughtered animal. What else can it mean?"

Ryan was shaking his head, no doubt trying to conjure up another explanation. Unwilling to wait for him to see what was obvious, she left him standing there and stormed down the stairs. In the front room, and started kicking the piles about, looking for her phone.

Her foot connected with something hard beneath a crumpled jacket. It was the gas stove and clay dish. Next to the mattress, she found the tin box Gerallt kept his tobacco and skins in. Patting the pocket of every item of clothing she saw, she found no phone.

"Where the fuck else would he have it?" she grumbled with rising frustration. She started using her hands to pick apart the piles, desperation increasing. But for what? What did she hope for? To find out what already seemed inevitable? She'd said it already. Everyone else invoked in that ceremony was dead. Why wouldn't Filip be?

Why wasn't *she*? Was that yet to happen? Or was she supposed to suffer in some other way?

Ryan stood in the hall, rubbing his cheek as though reeling from a slap of reality. "Did you find your phone?"

"No. But it has to be here. Maybe he hid it somewhere."

"Look around, Alma," Ryan swept his hand about. "He lived in this one room. Everything is in plain sight. His drugs paraphernalia...everything. He wouldn't have hidden a stolen phone. Maybe he sold it after all."

Alma stood up, trembling and heaving with exertion. "Do you have your phone? Try calling my old number."

Ryan sighed and did as she asked. He slumped as he held the phone to his ear, but after a moment, he looked up in surprise. "It's ringing."

Alma took a sharp breath and hurried into the hall, then froze, listening for a ringtone or a buzzing. There was nothing. Just the faint warbling in the earpiece of Ryan's phone. Eventually, even that ended with an abrupt beep and an automated message.

"I guess it's really not here then," she said, leaning against the wall and looking at her own hands with sudden disgust. If she hadn't known the water was disconnected, she'd have run into the kitchen and washed them.

"No," Ryan said, pocketing his phone. "But it's somewhere. Someone must be keeping it charged if it's still ringing after three days."

Alma exhaled slowly and looked at the broken front door creaking open under its own weight. Voices were coming up the road.

"It doesn't matter now. We won't get it back."

"The police probably have a way of..."

"It won't help." Alma straightened up and stood in front of Ryan, challenging him with her gaze like she'd done in his kitchen. "I don't have anything left. I don't know how to fight this. You can see, can't you? I'm not crazy. This is really happening."

For a moment she was braced for the sinking feeling if he tried to deny it. She was ready to turn and walk away.

176

But eventually, Ryan's head bobbed in hesitant agreement. He looked off to the stairs and closed his eyes.

"Yes. Yes, Alma. You must be right. I guess you were right all along. Scapegoat is real."

A lump formed in Alma's throat. To hear somebody else say it was both liberating and terrifying.

"I was wrong about something," she said. "I used to think I had weapons to keep him at bay. But maybe it was like you used to say, maybe all the spells and rituals have just given him power."

Ryan folded his arms and shifted uncomfortably. "Perhaps. It's not for me to say."

"Ryan, this isn't the time to be diplomatic. You're a priest. Don't they train you how to deal with this sort of thing?"

"No! It's not exactly an everyday duty."

"But the Church has procedures for dealing with demons, right?"

"Alma, this is getting beyond…"

"*Doesn't it?* The Church believes demons are real and has ways of fending them off. Is that true or isn't it?"

Ryan chewed his lip for a few seconds. "Yes. There are rites for exorcising demonic oppressions. But this doesn't exactly follow the…"

He stopped, and both of them turned towards the front door as a car pulled up outside with the white, blue and fluorescent yellow police colours.

"We have to go," Alma said, stepping towards the kitchen. "We can get onto the path through the back."

Car doors opened and closed outside, and there was some faint radio chatter. Ryan shook his head.

"You go. I'll tell the police I came here out of concern for Gerallt. You get yourself away from here quickly."

Alma baulked, but at the sound of the gate swinging, she knew she had no time to argue.

"Listen to me," she whispered as she backed away. "My weapons have failed me. I need you to try yours. I'm asking you to help me."

In an instant, Ryan's expression softened, looking at her the way he used to so many years ago.

"I'll try," he said. "Just go! I'll speak to you later."

Alma got to the back door just as there was knocking at the front. She opened it as quietly as she could, no louder than the conversation that was now taking place in the hall. It took her a moment to get her bearings and remember which side of the wooden fencing would take her onto the woodland path. Her heart was racing as she looked up at the windows of the house next door. Hopefully, any nosy neighbours would be distracted by what was happening out front.

It was not a graceful act, nor as quiet as she would have liked, but she managed to haul herself up and over the fence. Her foot caught a soft bank of dirt as she landed. She slid and fell onto the grass. There she remained, listening to the rushing of her own blood in her ears and the voices at the front of the house. Ryan sounded as composed and calm as ever.

Picking herself up, she made her way quickly onto the path leading into the woods, and towards the nearest safe place she could think of.

Chapter 17

The living room didn't look like the home of a university professor. Certainly not of someone with letters after his name. It was more Alma's expectation of a house share full of young male students, with handed-down furniture and DVDs and games controllers sitting out.

Damien walked in, his hair now neatly combed over and not flopping wildly like it had been when he'd answered the door. He was wearing a pair of track bottoms now too, instead of just boxer shorts.

"That's better. Sorry about that," he said. "I should have asked if you wanted a drink or something."

Alma politely declined and watched him take a seat on the couch opposite her. He clearly hadn't been planning to be anywhere today, and she could hear the fan of the games console whirring even though the screen was blank.

"I didn't plan on dragging you into this," she said. "But I don't trust the police to deal with it. I had to go to someone else."

Damien rubbed the side of his face. "I'm confused. Go back a step. What's actually happened?"

"I don't know for sure. But I stayed out last night, and I saw in the news this morning that Robyn was dead..."

"Wait? Robyn's dead?" Damien squinted at her, experimenting with a few different expressions before deciding on the one he thought was appropriate. "Where did you read about that?"

Alma had prepared for that question. "I saw it on social media. They didn't name her, but there was a picture of the building and when I called her, she didn't answer."

Damien already had his phone out, frantically scrolling through the pages of a news app. "I can't see anything about it. There's only stuff about that other girl they found in the woods."

"Oh, really?" Alma felt a frigid grip on her chest. What if it wasn't in the news yet? What if the police had kept it quiet while they investigated? How would she explain how she knew, when she'd already made it sound like she'd not been home? "I don't know why that would be."

Damien stood up and began pacing the room agitatedly, still thumbing his phone. "No, nothing at all. Is there a chance you could be mistaken? Let me try calling her."

Alma shrugged, feigning uncertainty while Damien made the call and got through to Robyn's voicemail. He put on a thin-lipped grimace as he hung up and peered at Alma.

"Maybe they recalled the story to avoid impeding the investigation," she suggested, well aware of how unlikely it sounded. "I don't know what's going on. I just know that I don't feel safe and I don't want to go back to the flat by myself."

It was mostly true. She didn't want to go back to that flat, alone or with anyone else, ever again. But that was where her belongings were and she didn't want to risk being seen walking through town.

Damien was only too willing to take pity. As he drove her towards the harbour, he still looked bleary-eyed from his all-night gaming session. He probably expected to get to the house and find Robyn alive and well. To find that it had all been a big misunderstanding.

As they neared Rheidol Terrace, she asked him not to park too close. He said nothing, but obliged by turning onto another side road. Alma's heart thumped as she tried to work out what she'd say if any police were at the flat.

The clouds shifted overhead as she got out of the car. An incongruous warmth touched her skin. Against all expectations, everything felt strangely normal. Damien walked beside her and she noticed right away that the door of the tattooist's shop was open. The buzzing of a tattoo gun came from inside. The gate to the flat courtyard was not sealed off with police tape. It swung open at Alma's touch. As soon as they passed into the small patio where the sun's gaze did not reach, Damien began humming to himself. Alma wondered if she was about to prove herself crazy.

"Doesn't look like a crime scene to me," Damien said, braving a chuckle. Alma silently ascended the wooden steps to the front door, where there was also no tape or any evidence the police had been there. Her key turned in the lock the same as ever. She tensed her hand, and she pushed the door open, looking into the hall.

Damien called out Robyn's name. Alma played along, calling out after him.

"It's just us, me and Damien. Are you here?"

"Maybe she's asleep?" Damien offered. "Has she been on nights this week?"

Of course, there was no answer. All the doors were closed, including the lounge. She'd come as far as she needed with Damien. He'd gotten her to the flat without being seen. He didn't need to become any more involved. She could handle the rest by herself.

"Yes," Alma replied weakly, stepping in. "She has been."

She put her ear against Robyn's door, but the whole time, her eyes were on the lounge door, and the small bursts where the tips of the nails had almost passed through.

She looked at Damien, willing the colour of embarrassment to her face and giving him a sheepish smile. "I'm so sorry. You must think I'm a complete basket case. She's in there sleeping."

"Don't apologise," Damien said, wearing the same smile he'd had when he thought he'd saved the day by finding her a place to live. "Robyn's not dead. That's a good thing."

"I must have seen something online about that other murder and...I don't know…"

Damien rushed forward and wrapped his arms around her before she could react. Alms went stiff, her focus still on the lounge door.

"It's OK," Damien said. "You're not mad, you're just traumatised from finding that girl's body. It's understandable."

He was holding her as though she might slip from his grasp or fall to pieces where she stood. She fought the instinct to push him away.

"You're right. I shouldn't have jumped to conclusions about Robyn not answering her phone. Thank you for coming here with me."

Damien released her, his hands sliding until they rested on her arms. He stooped to her eye level. "It's going to be fine. How about I stay and make us both a drink? You probably shouldn't be on your own today."

"That's very kind," Alma said, forcing one of the most difficult smiles of her life. "I'd happily invite you to stay, but I'm probably not thinking straight because I haven't slept. I just need to go to bed and sleep it off."

"Maybe," Damien said. One of his hands drifted up and pushed a strand of her hair behind her ear. An uncomfortable icy sensation beaded down her spine. "But I really don't think you should be alone..."

In a moment of horror, Alma realised that, if she could not get Damien to leave, then inviting him into her room might still be the lesser evil. Robyn was not in her room. And if she was still hanging from the lounge door, Alma had no explanation about how she'd known about it or why she'd lied about it.

"I'll be alright," she said, fighting to not recoil from his touch and trying to think of a way to send him off in good spirits. "I'll owe you a drink after work one day next week for this, OK?"

That seemed to have the desired effect. Damien's grin widened and he nodded emphatically. "Sure, it's a date."

Alma laughed in weary relief and Damien stepped back. Immediately, she folded her arms in front of her and watched as he walked out the front door. On the threshold, he stopped and looked back. "Get some rest, feel better, and give me a call if you need anything at all."

She smiled, nodded, and waited the minimum amount of time to close the door without seeming impolite. As soon as the creaky footsteps faded, she pulled out her phone and searched. Damien had been right. There was nothing in the news about the murder last night at all. Lifting her gaze, she opened Robyn's door and confirmed to herself that the room was empty. Next, she gently pushed at the lounge door, her stomach already roiling with fear. The door swung easily and without any apparent excess weight.

Taking a deep breath, she stepped through and walked several paces into the lounge, dimly lit by the glowing curtains, before turning around to face whatever was there.

Her insides fell within her. The body was gone. The door was only slightly blood stained. The nail-holes were prominent, the wood around them having pulled away under the weight of the body. A dark brown patch remained on the carpet.

She released her breath. She was trembling and felt weak. Everything she remembered had indeed happened here, but the primary evidence of it was gone. It had been dealt with and wiped away. The police had been and gone.

Ryan had taken care of it. If evil was still in this place, it was only because it was following her.

Whether Ryan could help her take care of *that* remained to be seen.

With no reason to linger, Alma went to her room and packed up all her things. It didn't take long; she'd scarcely begun to unpack since moving in. When everything was stuffed into her luggage case, she checked and found she still had no messages on her new phone. She stepped into the hallway and made a call.

"Where are you?" Ryan said as soon as he answered.

"I'm at my flat," Alma replied, before correcting herself. "My old flat. Robyn's flat."

"Why did you go there? That's a live crime scene!"

"I don't care. I needed to get my things. Anyway, it looks like the police have been and gone."

Saying it out loud reminded Alma how odd it seemed. The scene of a murder processed and left unattended in less than twenty-four hours.

Ryan sighed irritably. *"Alright, well, it's done now. Are you going to go back to the presbytery?"*

"Sure. Is that where you are?"

"No, I've only just finished with the police and now I have to go and prepare for another Mass. I'll be home this evening."

"Oh, right." Alma stood in front of the window and looked out over the courtyard. The bins didn't look like they had been disturbed. "Have you looked into what we talked about?"

There was a pause. *"You mean the exorcism rite? Sort of. I've got the liturgy, but...it's not the sort of thing you're supposed to do just off-the-cuff. There's a whole discernment process, and a bishop is supposed to agree..."*

"Ryan, it'll be fine. I trust you."

Another pause.

"It needs to be somewhere with a consecrated altar. There's a vigil at Welsh Martyrs tonight, so we can't go there."

"What about your old church? The one that was shut down."

"I don't have a key anymore."

185

Alma sucked in a frustrated breath. As much as she didn't want to believe it, she wondered if he was just making excuses. Then it came to her.

"You have a key for the chapel on the hill, don't you."

"I...yes, I do."

"It has an altar, which will presumably have been consecrated at some time."

"Of course."

"So? Will that work? Do consecrations have an expiry date?"

"No. The chapel on the hill will work fine. Good thinking."

"Great. When should I meet you there?"

"I can be there for seven thirty. Stay safe until then."

There was something about the way he said that: something that persuaded Alma he might just believe there was something she needed to keep safe from.

The call ended. Alma prepared to leave the room she'd not had time to come to think of as home. As she turned, she startled as yet again she was confronted with a hanging shape on the back of the door.

It was the dress Robyn had left for her. A lump grew in her throat as she thought about the last time they'd spoken. She covered her mouth and tried to gulp down the rising grief, but she choked and it came out as a shuddering wail. Her eyes squeezed closed, but not hard enough to stop the tears from flowing. She thought about the trust Robyn had shown so easily, and how she'd been rewarded with death for inviting Alma into her life: for being led into something that should have been uplifting and bonding.

Opening her eyes, she picked up the note that had accompanied the dress. A strangled laugh escaped her lips as she read it again. When she'd finished, her eyes scanned back up to the words: 'Promise me you'll save him'.

Promise me.

When the tightness in her lungs had subsided, and she was left with numb arms and an aching throat, Alma rubbed her eyes and took the dress down from the door.

Chapter 18

The wooden door issued a faint creak as it opened,
releasing the smell of damp wood, mildew and body
odour. A chill breeze rushed over Scapegoat's shoulders
and into the shed. A dark shape near the back scrambled
into an upright sitting position as best as it could with its
hands tied.

Scapegoat closed the door behind him and crouched in
front of the man, looking him down and up. He was a
pitiful sight: eyes wide in fear, too weak to struggle
against his bonds.

"If it's any consolation," Scapegoat said, "you were
never as close as you thought to saving her. You thought
you had power and control, but it was never going to be
enough."

His prisoner made no sound or movement. He simply
stared. Scapegoat chuckled and reached to pull the gag
from his mouth. The prisoner turned his face away at
first, but gasped with relief when his mouth was free.

"It's been a long time since we had this conversation,
hasn't it?" Scapegoat sneered. "I asked you not to get in
the way. But you really believed you were her protector,
sent from heaven, didn't you?"

"I was wrong," the prisoner whispered, his voice
cracked and dry. "I didn't want to dig all of this up again.
Please."

Scapegoat reached into the pocket of his long coat and
took out the lender knife. His prisoner flinched at the
sight, struggling vainly. The wind rattled the windows.

"What is it you think you are doing here?" Scapegoat
asked.

The man's eyes darted around the room, as though he might find the answer on one of the shelves. In the end, he simply closed his eyes tight. "I thought she needed me. Thought we were supposed to be there for each other.."

"No." Scapegoat shook his head. "I was the one who summoned you here. She never needed you. That's why she ran from you all those years. You could never be the one to keep her safe. You just wanted to believe that she needed you."

His prisoner shook his head frantically. Spittle flew from his mouth as he yelled. "You're wrong! She brought it all on herself because she ran! Because she didn't listen!"

"You know who she never tried to run from?" Scapegoat leaned in closer, holding the blade up towards his prisoner's face as he whispered, "*Me*."

There was a moment of stillness before the prisoner sagged, his body racked with sobs. "Fine. I'll go. It's over. I'm done. I don't want to be a part of this anymore."

Scapegoat grabbed a fistful of the man's jacket and pulled him to his feet. His shoes scraped noisily against the floor as he tried to stand on weakened legs.

"You won't be."

The clouds gathered tightly overhead, heavy with rain held like the breath of a pensive audience. Salted wind promised a miserable walk for any students coming down the hill. Black and white waves rushed inland, fleeing the looming storm. Alma hugged her jacket close to herself as she rounded onto the seafront and looked up the hill.

The skirt of the dress flapped against her legs, as if imploring her to go back. Squinting, she looked up to the little chapel on the hill and saw a light was on, signalling to her while the rest of the town ignored it. Her hand lifted to her pendants, but she could find no words for them. *Perhaps it was truer to say that they had no words for her.*

Residual light from the seafront clubs and what little moonlight filtered through the clouds illuminated the path up the hill. She watched her footing carefully, one hand holding her hair behind her head, grateful that at least the ground was dry for now. On her back, she felt the same pair of eyes watching her.

Good. Alma wanted him to see this. She felt oddly serene.

Ryan's car was parked outside the chapel. Yellow filament light glowed from the windows and through the gaps around the door, making the small stone building look like a life-sized illuminated Christmas village model. The car rocked slightly in the howling wind, but the chapel stood firm, enduring this storm as it had all others down the centuries.

Alma turned the iron ring on the door, and the latch on the other side lifted, and she stepped through. It was not warmer inside, but being out of the wind made it feel like it was. Ryan stood at the far end with a messenger bag, facing away from her and decanting items onto the altar.

"I'm almost ready," he said without turning. "There's a lot of the process we're cutting out. Technically, a bishop is supposed to discern if exorcism is necessary. Then there's supposed to be two priests."

"It's fine," Alma said, closing the door behind her, dulling the roar of the wind. A pew had been pulled forwards from one of the walls. A leather-bound book lay open at one end. She removed her jacket and draped it over the back. "All I need is for you to try."

Ryan sighed and turned around. His face changed as he saw her. His lips moved, as if readying themselves for the right words.

"You look amazing," he said eventually.

Alma felt a rush of warmth on her face, gave an appreciative smile and sat down on the pew. Looking about, she tried to imagine what Ryan came here to think about. It wasn't a comfortable space. More than anything, it felt empty. Forgotten. The two things she had found so inviting about her room in Robyn's flat. The difference now was that Ryan was here.

"What do you need me to do?" she asked.

Ryan approached, holding a small glass bottle with a clear liquid in it. He knelt down in front of the pew, directly in front of her. For the first time, his clerical collar gave him a reassuring professionalism, yet his eyes held a certain charming insecurity which had once upon a time made it so easy for her to trust him.

"Just lay down on the pew," he said. "The rules say you should be restrained. We'll forgo that part, I think."

"Thanks," Alma scoffed, turning sideways and easing herself down. The cold wood against her shoulders drew a gasp. "He's never taken control of my body to attack someone. Not as far as I know, anyway. Let's hope there isn't a first time for everything."

"You're being rather sportive about this, given the circumstances. You do know what this procedure is intended for, don't you?"

"I do. You're going to make Scapegoat leave me alone forever."

Staring at the ceiling, she heard Ryan unscrewing the lid of the bottle.

"Yes," he said. "I'm going to try to set you free of this oppression."

Alma closed her eyes and listened to the wind railing against the window at the end of the chapel. Something wooden rattled loudly at that end of the room. The sound chilled her more than the cold air. Her thoughts drifted back and forth. She wondered what the hell she was doing, but didn't know what else she could do.

"If this doesn't work," she asked, "are you going to tell me it was because I didn't have enough faith?"

"How much faith do you have?"

"In Christ, or in you?"

Ryan hesitated before answering. "The Church teaches that the efficacy of a sacrament is not dependent on the faith of the receiver. If this doesn't work, it'll be because there was no demon to exorcise."

"And it will be the Church's position that I'm just crazy. Wonderful."

"But not my position," Ryan said gently. Alma heard a soft flicking of his hand, and wrinkled her nose as spots of water landed on her face.

"God of heaven," Ryan began, "God of earth, God of Angels, God of Archangels, God of Patriarchs, God of Prophets, God of Apostles…"

Alma knit her fingers together over her stomach, like she was posing for her own funeral. It was from this hill that she'd felt those eyes watching her on that first day. She was no longer cornered in her own hiding place. She had come up to *his*.

"…God of Martyrs, God of Confessors, God of Virgins, God who has power to give life after death and rest after work…"

More titles than Alma had amulets on her chain. She locked her jaw and tried to drive away the scepticism washing over her like dirty water from a toppled bucket. She tried to remember how it had been so easy to listen to Gerallt's words on the night of the ceremony. *Tonight, it should be easier*, she told herself. *Gerallt did not know what he was dealing with. Ryan does.*

"From the snares of the devil, Deliver us, O Lord," Ryan went on. "We beseech You to hear us. That You may crush down all enemies of Your Church."

Through her eyelids, Alma saw shadows moving and realised Ryan was making the sign of the cross over her. She inhaled sharply, her lungs suddenly tight and her heart pounding. On the screen of her eyelids she saw the familiar visage materialising, grinning and bleeding from the neck.

"Depart, then, transgressor." Ryan spoke louder now. "Depart, seducer, full of lies and cunning, foe of virtue,

194

persecutor of the innocent. Give place, abominable creature, give way, you monster, give way to Christ, in whom you found none of your works. For he has already stripped you of your powers and laid waste your kingdom, bound you prisoner and plundered your weapons. He has cast you forth into the outer darkness, where everlasting ruin awaits you and your abettors."

His voice reverberated in the small chapel, even over the howling wind and the metallic trembling in the brass fixings and brittle leaded windows. Alma tried to release her breath, but found she could not. She felt something under the base of her throat, filling her chest.

Panicking, she shuddered and opened her eyes. Her lips moved, but there was no sound to make. She couldn't see Ryan. All she could see was the vaulted ceiling of the chapel, which appeared to fall away from her like an inverted chasm.

She sat up, pressing her hands into her midriff. The swelling in her chest yielded and escaped up her throat, exiting her mouth as a distraught cry.

In the next moment, the room was as she remembered. She shook and panted, the cold burrowing deeper into her skin. But as she turned her head, she saw Ryan, his smile calm, confident and triumphant.

"Are you alright?" he asked.

Alma turned herself, lowering her legs off the pew and finding the ground with her feet. The air in the room felt thin and vacant. If Scapegoat, the Holy Spirit or anyone other than Ryan and herself had been there, they were gone. It was just the two of them now.

"What happened?"

Ryan smiled and shuffled closer on his knees, settling a hand on her shoulder. "I finished the ritual. That's it. It's done. There's nothing more to do."

She imagined the things she'd visualised happening during an exorcism. Sounds of a wailing demon being cast back into hell. Windows shaking, objects flying about the room and other dramatic manifestations. Anything that would have proven beyond any doubt that a change had taken place.

Instead, there was only Ryan, looking at her like a doctor with good news. The same look that had meant so many different things down the years. He'd worn it as a boy every time he'd assured her it wasn't her fault he'd been beaten for her brother's prank. He'd worn it as a teenager when he swore that he wasn't judging her, but protecting her. Now he wore it without saying anything at all, brown eyes full of belief that it was going to be alright.

Shrugging his hand off her shoulder, Alma slid forwards off the pew, closing the gap and falling against his body and pressing her lips to his. Ryan caught her in his arms without a flinch. It was like muscle memory summoning the first kiss they'd shared a lifetime ago. The first time he'd told her she didn't need to be afraid, and she'd believed him.

She tried to make it last as long as she could, fending off every complication as it arose in her mind. The taste of his lips and the warmth of his arms she'd known years before he gave himself to the Church. As she slid her arms around his neck, even the chill in the air seemed to back away from her defiance.

196

Like a headsman's axe, reality fell upon her in the form of a phone ringing. It was Ryan's. He eased himself back, still gazing at her.

"It's going to be fine," he whispered. "This is...it will be fine. I should just..."

Alma nodded, not trusting her voice with any important words as his hand removed itself from her waist, and the chill pounced on her once again. She lowered her gaze to the stone floor and eased herself back onto the pew while he hurried towards the altar. When he got there, she was relieved at least that he did not fall to his knees in repentance. But the way he turned slowly with his phone in hand was scarcely more reassuring.

"It's the police," he said. "I'm not sure what they'd be calling me about now. I should call them back and find out."

"Of course," Alma forced a weak smile. "They'll still want to talk to me, too. Maybe we should just go down there and face the music."

"No, not yet." Ryan strode back to her and stooped. "I'll go to the car and talk to them now. They don't need to know you're with me. Just stay here, and when I'm done, we can work everything out."

"I thought you said there was nothing more to be done." Alma laughed silently. "Have I created more problems?"

Ryan smiled. His hand stroked her face, and the pangs of anxiety lifted in an instant. "Not problems, no. Give me ten minutes."

When he opened the door, the cold wind rushed in and carried him outside like a retreating wave. She strained to listen, but all she heard was his car door open and close. She still had no idea how to answer some of the questions she was going to have to face. Ryan might have exorcised the killer, but the police were still looking for someone.

Alma got to her feet and wrapped her arms around herself, pacing idly towards the altar at the back of the chapel. The space around it was cluttered, most of the furnishings had been pushed towards the back. Perhaps to make room for parishioners, or tourists, more likely. Or thinking priests seeking solitude.

The loud wooden rattling was still there. It was coming from a small door to the right of the altar. It seemed absurd that such a small building would have two doors, but apparently the builders decided the custom of the priest entering by a different way to the congregation could not be dispensed with.

The wind picked up again and drove hard against the door, battering it furiously. The noise was joined by a small whistling from a gap somewhere in the stonework above the window. Something else too: a coarse, intermittent humming coming from the other side of the apse.

Her skin bristled as she moved around the altar. The noise was coming from a full-height cabinet with a dark wood door. The brass keyhole had a small key left in it. The humming came again: two short pulses, like a phone on vibrate mode. She looked towards the door. Ryan had only been gone a couple of minutes. Talking to the police would not be a quick affair.

She turned the key in the lock, intending only to peek inside and see if there was a phone. But as soon as the latch retracted, the door swung outward. Alma cried out as a naked male figure lurched towards her, an arm held above its head. She tried to leap back, but the man fell onto her, catching her off balance, and the two of them tumbled to the floor. Instinctively, she brought one arm up in front of her face defensively and pushed the man away.

The figure gave no resistance, but flopped off her limply. Alma scrambled up and grabbed a candlestick from the altar, wielding it in both trembling hands. But the man remained face down where he landed, his face obscured by unkempt wavy hair. *No. Impossible. It couldn't be happening again. Not so soon after it was meant to be over.*

She thought about running outside to get Ryan. But if he was talking to the police, she'd give away that she was with him. *Fuck!* Fighting to steady her breath, she leaned down and tugged at the man's shoulder, turning him over as she kept the candlestick raised, poised and ready. At the sight of the face, her stomach twisted so hard she thought she might be sick. It was Filip's haunted face, the front of his body smeared with blood from a slit in the base of his throat.

The howling wind disappeared completely underneath Alma's anguished scream. She dropped the candlestick as all strength left her, and she sank to the ground, clutching frantically at her hair. She'd been right. Scapegoat had got to everyone she'd named in her prayer. All her efforts were too late.

The two pulses sounded again behind her. She turned and crawled towards the cabinet on trembling arms. A plastic carrier bag hung from a screw in the back containing something large and bulky. That was where the sound was coming from. Breathing heavily through her teeth, she ripped the bag off the hook and upended it.

The large object inside fell to the floor with a thud — along with some sheets of paper — and Alma froze as she found herself staring into the vacant eyes that had haunted her nights for so many years. A mask in the form of a goat's head. The same face which had glared at her in the shower a few nights ago.

Her hand was shaking uncontrollably as she prodded it, expecting it somehow to come to life. It turned slightly and continued staring at the wall. She turned over the papers and saw that they were flyers for the Aberystwyth Wiccan Society, just like the one she'd taken from the Arcana shop. The wind returned, the side door rattled angrily, and something inside the mask buzzed twice. Alma tilted the mask and saw a phone inside it. A phone with a cracked screen showing a low battery warning.

It was *her* phone.

Cold hands were wringing her lungs like a damp flannel, and her eyes welled up as she examined the phone. There were a lot of angry messages from Filip. But there was also one message *to* Filip, sent as if by her, the day after she lost her phone.

'I'm with Ryan now in Aberystwyth. He's keeping me safe the way it always should have been. The way you couldn't.'

Reading the following messages, it became clear that Filip, in his fury, had taken the bait. The goat mask stared up at her from the floor, the vacant eyes inanimate and without threat. Just a mask. A mask worn by someone who had written that message from her phone.

Alma held her breath, as if making the slightest noise would summon the danger again. Scapegoat — he wasn't gone at all. He really had been there all along…

200

A swathe of cold gripped her shoulders, the wind roaring as the main door opened. She threw the phone towards the cupboard reflexively. But the naked body of Filip still lay in plain sight. She rose and turned sharply, her knees almost too weak to lift her. Ryan stood in the doorway, his hair dishevelled and his mouth agape.

"What are you doing with him?" he asked. "What were you looking for?"

"Ryan, please tell me this isn't what it looks like," she whimpered. "Tell me you didn't kill my brother."

Ryan took two steps forward, but stopped as soon as Alma picked up the candlestick and brandished it. His eyes still had a lingering confidence that would have been comforting, but for his lack of surprise.

"Of course I did, Alma," he said. "There's no point denying it. I'd hoped you wouldn't have to know. I'd hoped we wouldn't have to come here at all. But we did what needed to be done."

Once again, between herself and a priest, Alma found herself questioning her own sanity. He spoke so calmly that she couldn't help but want to believe that it would all make sense, if only she would listen.

"You told me you were going to help me be rid of Scapegoat. You told me you believed he was real. Was any of that true?"

"Scapegoat is real enough." Ryan laughed. "And we got rid of him tonight. Evil spirits aren't creatures that come for us while we sleep. They are the lies we put our trust in. Tonight was about helping you to put your trust where it belonged. And it worked. You do understand that, don't you?"

"Oh, Jesus…what are you saying, Ryan? What about Claire Warwick? Robyn? Gerallt? Did you kill them too?"

Ryan's smile faltered, and he plunged his hands into the pockets of his long coat. "I'm sorry it turned out like this. This wasn't the way I meant for it to go at all."

"What, you didn't mean to murder a bunch of people who'd done nothing wrong?"

"Come on, Alma. Filip was far from innocent."

"But what about the others? What did they do?"

Ryan chewed his lip and took another step closer. Alma tightened her grip on the candlestick.

"Sometimes people suffer not only for the things they themselves do," Ryan said darkly. "You suffered because of your brother's actions all your life. I took a serious beating because of what he did to you that night. You and I understand this better than most."

"So, what? You pretended to be Scapegoat just so that you could make me believe he was back for real? And you could make me think you'd exorcised him?"

"Alma, *we* are Scapegoat. You and I. Suffering for someone else's sin. We should have been each other's strength. I always tried to be there for you…"

"You killed innocent people!"

"I know. It's a shame. But this all happened because you put your faith in the wrong place. But there is a redemptive value to suffering. After tonight, it was all going to be over. Nobody else would have to suffer."

Alma raised the candlestick. Her eyes were so thick with tears she could hardly see him. "Get out of my way, you fucking psycho. You're a worse monster than Filip ever was. He didn't kill anyone! Forget about his sins. You're going to pay for your own."

"You and I would have become each other's refuge. The way it should always have been." Ryan shook his head, and his hand emerged from his pocket, holding a slender ten-inch knife. Alma felt a wave of dizzying, sickly fear course through her body. "I suppose I should have known it would never work out. Fate has always conspired to lead you away from me. I'm sorry that it ended up like this. I mean that, Alma."

She fixed her eyes on the knife as he paced towards her. A sharp pain at the base of her throat summoned her left hand to clasp it, as if to stem a wound. The blade was long and thin, designed to puncture...

With a strangled cry, she swung the candlestick towards Ryan's arm. He tried to spin away, but she was quick and the heavy base of the candlestick caught his hand. He bellowed in pain and dropped the knife. The door was still open at the far side of the room, and Alma used her momentum to barge past and get to it. She was so focused on her escape that when she felt herself grabbed around the torso, she pulled away a couple of times before realising that she could not free herself. A voice she could scarcely believe was Ryan's hissed in her ear.

"Running away from me, just when I thought you were ready to be saved. Same as always."

Alma dipped her head, looking for the blade of the knife and expecting to feel its hot bite. As Ryan pulled her around, she spotted it on the floor. In an act of desperation, she quickly whipped her head back. Nauseating pain flooded her senses, just as the crunch of Ryan's nose filled her ears. His grip did not loosen as she's hoped. Instead, he whirled around and pushed her towards the back of the chapel. She wasn't prepared, and staggered forwards, tripping on Filip's body and crashing to the floor, narrowly missing her head on the edge of the altar.

The periphery of her vision was crumbling as her head throbbed. She scrambled around the altar and looked back. Ryan had the knife in his hand again. The bottom half of his face was streaked with blood. This time, however, he did not move towards her. He stood in the middle of the nave, adopting a wide stand and moving back towards the door. She couldn't get past him and he knew it.

"You don't have to do this, Ryan," she yelled. "You don't have to make this any worse than it already is."

"It's too late." Ryan wiped his mouth with the back of his hand, leaving a grizzly smear. "Everything I've worked for is spoiled. You wouldn't let me be the one to save you. You were always too busy chasing your own destruction. So it's fine, I'll give you what you want. I won't let you be the ruin of me, too."

Alma looked for something else to use as a weapon. There was another candlestick on the altar, but she had no confidence in getting another lucky strike on him with something so cumbersome with her numb, trembling hands. He was almost at the main entrance, and would have plenty of time to anticipate her move.

Another gust of wind picked up. There was a rattling to her left. *The other door.* She couldn't see a lock on it. There was only a latch. Sucking in a breath, she lunged for it. The latch ring twisted and she yanked the door. It didn't move, stuck as though it had been sealed up somehow. She cried out and pulled with all her might. After a couple of tries, it started to shift, and then opened, spilling her out into the dark maelstrom. She stopped to close the door behind her, but the latch bar caught on the front of the cradle, bouncing off. There was no handle on the outside to lift it.

Not wasting another moment, Alma turned and found herself looking directly at the cliff edge. Beneath it, the roiling sea faded away into the dark blue of the night. Quickly she tried to orientate herself, locating the road on the other side of the chapel. Ryan was standing there, poised and armed. Alma's stomach churned like the waves below as she realised her situation was unchanged. Whichever way she tried to get around the chapel, he would intercept her.

Her hair lashed at her face, forcing her to squint and turn her head. There was no escape. Not from the wind. Not from Ryan. She looked down at the lights of the town and the animated neons of the nightclub on the pier. She still had breath in her lungs to scream for help, but nobody would hear.

Ryan made no move. He was waiting, not about to give her space to dash around the other way. He lifted his face menacingly. Alma saw the blood running down his neck from his broken nose. With one blow, she had erased every trace of the young man she'd wanted to trust.

The driving sea wind assailed her mercilessly, slowly sapping the last of her resistance. Her bare arms and shoulders stung from the cold. Her breathing became quick and shallow. All feeling was being flayed from her body until she was numb even to the fear.

She looked at the chapel, remembering how the window had looked different during the day: how the little door hadn't seemed so small when the young boy had been standing against it. Using it as a marker.

As long as you line up with the door and the flat bit....

Alma's breath caught in her throat. She took a step towards the chapel, feeling eyes on her. Had they really been his eyes all along? Reaching the door, she looked over her shoulder towards the cliff.

"That's it, go back to your brother," Ryan called out. "He's about as likely to help you now as he ever was."

Alma could see the smooth section of the ridge the boy had pointed out. She could also see the white trim of the fierce waves further out, whipped up and thrashed by the storm. It bore no resemblance to the sea she'd looked out upon from here last time. It was death.

She let out a long, ragged sob, expunging the last of the fear and hopelessness from herself. And then she pushed away from the door, sprinted, and leapt.

Chapter 19

The viciously cold water raked her skin like clawing
rats. Her legs screamed as she kicked and threw her arms
towards the streetlights of the promenade that
disappeared and reappeared with each swell. Each time
the water recoiled behind her, she couldn't tell if she was
closer or further away.

Desperately, she willed herself towards the shore and
kicked. Nothing around her seemed to move besides the
water. The town ahead was like a flat backdrop in a video
game, never getting closer or further away, never really
even there.

A powerful surge pulled her head under. For a moment,
there was nothing but peaceful rumbling in her ears, as if
she could simply wait and the biting cold and burning
pain would just pass.

She broke the surface, and the blistering wind howled in
her ears once more. With waning strength, she grasped
hopelessly at the water. Suddenly, her knee crashed
painfully against a stoney surface. Crying out in anguish
and relief, she clawed at pebbles. Her foot found
purchase, and she scrambled up the beach, out of the
grasping waves and into the icy embrace of the night air.

Her eyes darted to the cliff rising above her, blinking
away the stinging salt water in her eyes. She was too
close to see the chapel, or anyone who was up there.
Turning the other way, she saw the lights of the pier
nightclub further along the otherwise sleeping seafront. It
didn't seem too far away until she started running up the
beach and found her legs had almost no strength in them.
The wet, clinging satin of her dress was like a magnet to

the air chill, making the seaward wind feel like an army of demons lashing her with barbed whips.

Shaking and gasping, she clambered her way up the beach. The pier now seemed like a distant mirage, unreachable. Her legs felt brittle and liable to snap beneath her at any moment. She counted the last few paces to the concrete steps leading up to the road.

As she climbed the steps, the wind howled the indignance of the waves at her escape. As soon as her head rose above the level of the road, she saw a pair of lights coming down the hill from the church. Car headlamps approaching fast.

Frantically, she looked around for somewhere to hide. Not back down to the beach — that was precisely where Ryan would look. To the left, the dark expanse of the Old College building was unlit and lifeless, no doubt locked up tight. To her right, there was the street leading up the hill. She wouldn't get far that way.

As she hesitated, trying to pick a direction to run and hope for the best, she spotted a sign on the corner of the street. *Arcana*. She recalled going in there the first time, and the shop owner's angry words to his assistant.

As the sizzling headlights swerved down from the castle hill, Alma charged across the street at a full sprint. With the air whipping at her, it felt like running with a hail of arrows falling on her back. She ignored the pain and focused on the door with the peeling paint and the window filled with flyers.

When she slammed against it, the door flew open, eschewing its rotted frame with a screech. Once again, she plunged into near blackness. She careened into a shelf, and several glass items tumbled and shattered on the floor. *Yes!* Maybe someone lived upstairs and they would hear. Before her eyes adjusted to the dark, she lashed out at the shelf again, sending more delicate items crashing onto the ground. All she could think about was that if she caused enough damage and made enough noise, someone would come to stop her.

A yellow sliver of light crept across the ceiling from outside. Alma froze. No sound came from upstairs. All was silence but for the wind outside and the tires on the road as a car passed.

Alma shook violently. It was as though the cold night had its hooks into her and would not let go. The water dripping from the hem of her dress stung her calves like needles. She went back to the door and shoved hard against it with her shoulder.

The door shoved back. Hard. It cracked against her head and sent her sprawling away. She crashed into the shelf and landed on her side. The floor dug into her arm with a brittle crunch of broken glass, and the hot flow of blood awoke her chill-numbed skin.

Through the haze of pain, she saw Scapegoat briefly backlit by the streetlights, before he slammed the door shut. His staring, slot-pupiled eyes were once again alive with malice. Alma pushed herself up and planted her palm into more glass. The ground itself was clawing at her as she scrambled further into the room. The opening to the back of the shop was dark, but she remembered Dewi calling up some stairs. There would be a way up.

As she moved, she shouted for help and swiped at the displays, sending more stock crashing to the floor. Her hand connected with something heavy and round. Without looking back, she hurled it and heard it impact against a body. The cries of her own voice drowned out the footsteps behind her, so that she didn't know how close they were until a hand clamped onto the back of her neck. A violent push propelled her into the counter. Her hip connected with the corner of the reinforced glass, and a shriek of pain ripped from her lungs.

Hopelessly, Alma slumped to the floor, but fingers closed around her throat and lifted her, turning and pinning her against the counter. Even in the darkness, she could make out the haunting features of Scapegoat's face. She swung a fist up into the crook of his elbow. His arm buckled, but he lunged forward and pressed his entire weight against her. The edge of the counter dug into the small of her back, and she had no more space to lash out.

"Don't do this!" she choked, grabbing at his coat and vainly trying to push him off her. Scapegoat squared up his stance, released her throat, and instead clasped a fistful of her hair. He wrenched her head back, and Alma felt his eyes on her exposed throat. Her shivering and torn arms and hands were suddenly forgotten. None of those things were going to be her death.

"Look at me, Alma." The voice was barely recognisable, muffled and resonant beneath the mask. "This is the face of the fear and mistrust you used to push everyone away. This is the face of your brother's sin. This is the face of the evil you embraced to try to save yourself."

"That's not...*ah!*" A vicious yank of her hair silenced her.

"This is the face of your prayer to every idol asking to be left alone. And this is the face that is going to give you everything you prayed for."

There was a glint of steel, and Alma watched the knife raise and disappear under her chin. All feeling drained away as her body awaited the kiss of the blade against her throat. The terrible anticipation was agonising. She looked up at Scapegoat's face for a clue as to when to expect it.

Scapegoat was breathing heavily, exertion and pain present there. Despite the face, there was a human voice in there, and for the first time Alma felt acutely aware that the mask and the person wearing it were distinct from each other.

"You can't hurt me," she said. "He'll save me. Ryan is here. He's keeping me safe."

"He was here," the reply came from beneath the unmoving mouth. "But you chose to run from him."

"I know I did." Alma shook her head, blinking hard until she felt the flow of tears. "I'm sorry."

"Everyone is sorry when they have no other choice. Saying sorry didn't spare me a beating that night. Do you think it will spare you now?"

"I'm sorry that happened to you." Alma's throat was so tight she could hardly project the words. "I'm sorry for everything."

"I could listen to you say it a thousand times. But it's not enough. It's never enough."

Alma pulled back stiffly, taking a deep breath and holding it, as though it were her very life. A calm lucidity washed over her.

"I ran because I was scared," she said. "But I don't want to be scared. Please, Ryan. Help me to not be scared anymore."

The grip on her hair relaxed. The mask floated before her, silent, as though the spirit animating it was fading. A human hand came up, still holding the blade, and pulled the mask away, revealing Ryan's face. His gaze was detached and impassive, like he was hearing a confession and forcing himself to betray no emotion.

"It's much too late for that," he said with a voice that was cold and pragmatic. "Everything I tried to do for you is ruined. There's no coming away from this. Because of you, Scapegoat is what I've become. As long as you're still here, I'll always be…"

The knife returned to Alma's neck.

"No!" Alma gasped and shook her head rapidly. "I brought this on us! I'll fix it! I promise. I'm ready to trust you."

She swallowed her trepidation as she slowly craned her face up to gaze at him. Her throat pressed gently against the knife deferentially. The blade yielded and withdrew until she was close enough to touch her lips to his. Pain and fear coursed through her veins, but she forbade herself to tremble.

Ryan lowered the knife. When she pulled her head back, he was staring at her with confusion written all over his face.

"You're ready to let me save you?" he mumbled.

Alma nodded wordlessly. A quiet gasp escaped her lips as Ryan replaced the knife into his coat and buttoned the pocket closed. He still had her pressed against the counter, but his weight against her body now had a very different implication.

"We should go," Alma whispered. "Let's go somewhere safe together, shall we?"

In a moment of silence, she was uncertain if Ryan had even heard her. He was staring at her mouth, like the words were still on her lips and he was examining them for truth.

"No," he said. "We need to finish what we began. It's not done yet."

The hand which had grasped her hair coiled around her waist and hoisted her up to sit on the counter. Ryan pushed against her and tilted his head.

"I thought you said everything was done?" She failed to keep the tremor from her voice.

"*My* part was done. I want to finish what *you* started."

His words were a prelude to a kiss she knew was coming. His mouth found hers hungrily, and she had to plant her hands down behind to stop herself falling back. Her throat was still clenched with fear, and she wondered if he could taste it on her. She lifted a hand — bringing it up high so he could not suspect she was going for the knife in his pocket — and slipped it over his shoulder and around his neck.

Ryan's hands were frantic and feverish. The touch of his fingertips was piercing cold through the wet satin, as was the glass surface of the counter. He tugged and pulled at her as roughly as the stormy waves; she once again felt as though she was being pulled under, to her doom.

Alma's free hand gripped the back edge of the counter. Her fingertips curled into the space underneath it. She closed her eyes and pictured the counter as she had seen the first time. Leaning further back, her lips disengaged from Ryan's and she ran her fingers into his hair, guiding his face down onto her neck. She focused on sucking air in and out of her lungs, gasping like a person drowning and exhaling in a mimicry of lust.

The only heat she felt was from Ryan's mouth as it roved down her neck, giving her space to lean further back. She cupped his head as his mouth moved down to her chest, and her other hand slipped further down behind the counter. Her fingers touched the rim of an open box. Her heart pounded, and she forced out a quiet moan to disguise the true reason. At the limit of her reach, she panted to cover the scraping as she pulled the box closer to the edge. It was heavy with several objects which would spill out noisily if she pulled it too far.

Suddenly, Ryan pulled her hips forward, and Alma had to quickly grip the back of the counter to balance herself. Ryan hurriedly pushed the skirt of the dress up her legs. She gripped the back of his head, keeping his face pressed against her chest. Leaning further back was a convincing concession to his advance and allowed her to reach further under the counter until she touched a handle covered with soft hair.

"All I ever prayed for," she said breathily, eyes fixed upwards in concentration, "was for Scapegoat to leave me alone."

Ryan stilled and lifted his head to meet her gaze. His shoulders were heaving, and his arms gripped her rapaciously as he rasped his words out. "You're finally going to have what you prayed for."

Alma locked her jaw and nodded. "I know."

Shrugging off the numb sensation and allowing the fear to flood back and fuel her actions, she lashed her arm up from behind her.

She heard a squelch. Ryan's expression switched to pained shock as the blade of the goat-foot handled athame dagger entered his throat. A wet groan issued from his open mouth, and his hand grabbed her arm.

Baring her teeth, Alma cried furiously and pulled down with a nauseating rip. Her eyes closed as blood sprayed across her face. Ryan's weight fell away from her, and she rolled to the side, swinging her legs down onto the floor. She backed away, knife held out in front of her.

But Ryan wasn't approaching. He was slumped on his knees, both hands under his chin, mouth open, gurgling softly. He looked up at her, but his eyes were as vacant and unseeing as the mask's. After a moment, he toppled and came to a rest against the counter. His hands dropped into his lap, and there was no more sound apart from the front door juddering against the wind, and drops of blood tapping onto the wooden floor in front of Ryan.

Alma placed the dagger on the counter and stumbled away until Ryan's body was out of sight, which was when her strength failed her. She fell onto her hands and knees, pain lancing up from her bleeding palms. Burying her face between her arms, she listened to the howl and sobbing that seemed to come from somewhere else in the room, but her body was shuddering so much, she knew it was her.

Outside, the storm continued to rage as though it didn't know what had happened. Like it was waiting for only one person to emerge. Alma pushed herself up and tested her legs until she found the resources to stand. Slats of streetlight fell across her from around the window displays. Her forearms were smudged red where her face had pressed into them. Her voice was spent entirely, but she wouldn't need it to tell the first person who saw her that she needed help.

She pulled the front door open, and the sea raged at her. Stepping outside and bracing herself against the wind, she looked up at the hill, presenting her bloodied face to the eyes which had watched from up there. But they weren't watching anymore.

The distant lights of the nightclub on the pier were sharp and painful. Alma squinted against them and shrugged off the angry lashing of the wind as she began walking.

Chapter 20

"Hello? Excuse me? Are you awake?"

Alma opened her eyes. The grey morning scrolled by to the rumble of the train. Overlaid onto it was her own reflection, looking back at herself, less pale and ghostly for the flowering bruise on her forehead. Over her shoulder, the kind-eyed face of the old Chinese woman in the seat next to her was hovering pensively.

A hot pain splashed across her arm as the woman's hand shook it to get her attention. Alma turned leaned away, wincing and hissing.

"I'm sorry, did I hurt you?" the woman asked, confusion and concern etching her face.

"No, it's fine." Alma forced a smile, rubbing her jacket sleeve. "I scraped it a few days ago. Still a bit sore."

"Oh, I didn't realise. It's just that you said you were changing at Shrewsbury, and it's the next stop."

Alma looked at her phone and saw that it was almost half past seven. She must have fallen asleep soon after the train had departed Aberystwyth.

She thanked the woman and eased herself to her feet. She still hurt in so many places. Dragging her bag into the vestibule, she wondered what was in it that was so heavy. The clothes in the bottom had not seen the light of day since she'd left Manchester. And now she was on her way back.

The train leaned into a turn, and she rested against the bulkhead with her unhurt arm. She noticed the Chinese woman standing behind her, smiling and holding something out towards her.

"I noticed you like protection charms?" The woman said, flitting her gaze to Alma's neck. "I'd like you to have this one. It's very good luck."

She was presenting a small obsidian coin pendant on a leather thong with a Chinese character etched onto it. Alma lifted her hand to touch the heavy bundle of pendants around her neck, unsure when she'd last given a thought to it. She didn't even recall putting it on that morning.

"That's very kind," Alma smiled. "Why don't you keep it? I think I have too many."

The woman kept smiling and did not retract her arm. Alma started to wonder if she ought to take the gift just to end the awkward moment, when the woman finally pocketed the pendant. Her laugh sounded false.

"Can never have too much luck, I think. Don't miss your stop."

The woman returned to the seating area. She was small and frail looking, but she appeared strangely unaffected by the heave of the stopping train that sent Alma grabbing for a handhold to keep herself upright.

The doors slid open, and half a dozen people on the platform watched Alma lift her bag down and out of the way before they filtered onto the train. Nobody else was getting off. Alma wasn't sure why she noticed that, but she did. It gave her an odd comfort. Nobody else who had been where she had been was going where she was going.

The train pulled away, and Alma watched the timetable screen. Her onward train was in half an hour, going from the same platform. The air was cold and crisp. The corrugated plexiglass panels in the pyramid-shaped

218

canopies over the platform scattered the daylight in uneven streaks on the ground, making it look wet. Alma shivered and hoped that thirty-two minutes would go by as quickly as the last three days.

Had it really been three days? Each one seemed not to have even begun. No waking with a start. No panics or nightmares. Nothing more to be scared of. Peaceful. The days and evenings had been different, as she gave difficult answers to simple questions. Perhaps there would be more difficult questions after the police realised she was gone. But that was a concern for another day.

A light drizzle began, playing the plexiglass like a marching drum. The platform filled up around her with commuters. Closing her eyes, she heard the shuffling of thirty or forty pairs of feet, rustling coats, and people coughing into hands. Yet she felt not a single pair of eyes on her.

Four trains came and went, and Alma inched her way nearer to the edge of the platform. Her train was next. There was a tiny clinking sound in her ear. She glanced about for a moment, trying to locate it, until she realised it was the sound of her own hand fidgeting with her pendants. Her thumb was pressing on the large Benedictine Cross that now seemed bulkier than all the others.

'The train now approaching platform 4 is the 9:12 service to Manchester Piccadilly'

Setting her bag down beside her, she reached behind her head and unclasped the chain. She bunched it up in her hand and closed her fingers around it, feeling the various shapes digging into her skin. Her entire body immediately felt lighter.

219

A distant rumbling grew. The train arrived and squealed to a halt. The doors opened. Nobody stepped out. Nobody around her got on, either.

"...please mind the gap..."

Alma looked down at the space between the platform and the train. She lowered her hand outwards and opened her fist. The chain and the pendants fell and disappeared into the gap. She listened until she heard the patron saint of protection against evil clink onto the stones below.

Then she stepped onto the train.

The End.

The author hopes you have enjoyed Do You Get What You Pray For and thanks you for taking a punt on an indie author! If you liked this book, the best way to show your appreciation is to leave a rating or review on Amazon and/or Goodreads.

You can also check out O. R. Lea's near-future science fiction thriller Riebeckite, the first of the Bruised Moon sequence, available on Amazon Kindle and in paperback.

O. R. Lea's website is orlea.co.uk, and you can follow him @orleaauthor on Twitter and Instagram.

Printed in Great Britain
by Amazon

87358745R00130